Brains

Brains

a
zombie
memoir

ROBIN BECKER

An Imprint of HarperCollins*Publishers*

HarperCollins books may be purchased for educational, business, or sales promotional use. For information please write: Special Markets Department, HarperCollins Publishers, 10 East 53rd Street, New York, NY 10022.

FIRST EDITION

Eos is a federally registered trademark of HarperCollins Publishers.

Designed by Paula Russell Szafranski

Library of Congress Cataloging-in-Publication Data

Becker, Robin, M. 1967–
   Brains : a zombie memoir / Robin Becker. — 1st ed.
     p. cm.
  ISBN 978-0-06-197405-2
  1. Zombiism—Fiction. 2. Zombies—Fiction. 3. Viruses—Fiction.
4. Resistance—Fiction. I. Title.
  PS3602.E295B73 2010
  813'.6—dc22
                               2009040569

10 11 12 13 14 OV/RRD 10 9 8 7 6 5 4 3 2 1

All goes onward and outward . . . and nothing collapses, And to die is different from what any one supposed, and luckier.

WALT WHITMAN, "SONG OF MYSELF"

PROLOGUE

WHAT YOU HOLD in your hands is a zombie memoir, the touching postlife story of a walking corpse and his journey toward self-acceptance and knowledge, told honestly and in the first person, straight from his skeletal hand to your plump one.

What you hold in your hands I wrote and left on top of the desk in my hideout, a log cabin in the northern wilds of Canada. It is nothing short of revolutionary. Revisionist historians, prepare to revise.

In life, I was an English professor at a small college in rural Missouri. My mind retained information like a steel trap: No one played six degrees of Bacon better than I. No one knew more about Walt Whitman, the New Testament, or B movies from the 1950s. In conversation, I relentlessly sought the upper hand, whether discussing the best method for making flaky piecrusts (use Crisco, not butter) or the cultural importance of Freud (as massive as his cigar).

In death, I am a flesh-eating zombie with a messianic complex and these superpowers: I can think and I can write.

My name is Jack Barnes and I am a survivor. This is my story.

CHAPTER ONE

BRAINS. AFTER I was resurrected, my first thought was, Brains. I want brains. Give me brains!

The imperative seemed to come from outside of my body; it rang in my head like the voice of a god I had no choice but to obey. Brains: I heard it clearly, simply, plainly. Brains! And I immediately set out to procure some.

Now that I have analyzed this hunger, this twisted form of cannibalism, I realize it does not reside in my stomach, the typical seat of appetite; it stems from a deeper place, my divine core, what some might call the soul.

It is a small price to pay for immortality.

Brains. More dear to me than my wife. More precious than my intellect and education, my Volvo and credit rating—all that mattered in "life" now pales in comparison to this infinite urge. Even now, as I write these words, my lips quiver and a drop of saliva—tinged crimson—falls onto the paper, resulting in a brain-shaped stain.

Stain, brain, rain, brain, pain, brain, sustain, brain, wane, brain, refrain, brain, cocaine, brain, main, brain, brain, brain, brains!

Oh, how I love them.

THE VIRUS HIT the world like a terrorist attack.

Lucy and I—both still warmly human—were holed up in the living room watching news reports of the zombie invasion. It wasn't confined to the Midwest, as they originally thought, but had spread all over the United States. Indeed, all over the world. And it happened in a matter of hours.

Brian Williams looked wan, scared, a little boy in a grown-up suit, the endearing humor in the corners of his eyes lost forever. Lucy clicked over to Fox. I always suspected my wife of secret conservatism, but I said nothing. Because there was Geraldo Rivera, out in the street, interviewing a she-zombie. A zombette.

"Why are you doing this?" Geraldo asked the creature. "Can you even talk? Everyone thinks you're a monster."

The zombie groaned and grabbed the reporter's cheeks as if to move in for a kiss.

"That zombie must've been an athlete in life," I said. "She's quicker than some of the others I've seen."

"The poor dear," Lucy said.

Geraldo bludgeoned the zombette with his microphone, but to no effect. The mic merely sank into the undead's head, disappearing like a baby thrown into quicksand. Geraldo wrestled it out and the camera zoomed in; the mic was covered with tufts of hair and bits of gore. Geraldo shook it like a rattle and the zombie struck, biting his hand. Geraldo shrieked—high-pitched, girlish—and Fox cut back to the newsroom, where a generic blonde warned viewers of the dangers of conversing with corpses.

"Now that's the kind of reporting I expect from Fox," I said. "Stating the obvious with bimbotic style."

"Do you think they could be here?" Lucy asked, her eyes darting around the room. "In our town?"

"Of course not," I said. "We're in the middle of the middle of nowhere. The flyover zone. No one comes here if they don't have to, not even dead people."

I heard a noise, as if Hook Man were scratching at our roof. I turned off the idiot box and threw open the drapes.

Lucy and I were surrounded; there were zombies at the windows, zombies at the doors, zombies coming down the chimney like Santa Claus. It was just like the movies.

That's the genius of George Romero. His initial trilogy—*Night of the Living Dead, Dawn of the Dead, Day of the Dead*—was prescient in the grand tradition of science fiction becoming fact. First you have to imagine a man on the moon, then you can put one there. Imagine an atom-splitting bomb, and then build one. Imagine a virus that turns corpses into the walking dead, and someone, somewhere, will develop that virus.

And now let us bow our heads in honor of Dr. Howard Stein, my creator. Our father. Mad Scientist Extraordinaire. God in the Garden of Evil. Daddy of the Undead. Cue maniacal laughter.

There was a crashing sound as zombies broke the living room picture window and stumbled in. I threw the remote at them. Nothing. Then the *TV Guide*. Nothing. A vintage 1950s kidney-shaped ashtray bounced off of one like a rubber ball. Finally, my copy of the *The Da Vinci Code,* never read. The ghouls kept coming.

"Their heads," Lucy yelled. "The news said you have to injure their heads!"

"You think I don't know that? It's a trope of the genre."

"Don't talk to me like I'm one of your students, Jack. It's demeaning."

As I bickered with my wife, my neighbor reached me. He was in his bathrobe and boxers and his feet were bare, the veins and bones bulging. The whites of his eyes were yellow and watery, and his arms were open wide for a hug. He leaned forward as if to tell me a secret.

And bit me. Just like that. Right on top of my shoulder, deep in the muscle.

It felt like a hot poker on my flesh, a rabid squirrel attack, the blinding light of a comet. It felt, in short, like sharp human teeth ripping me apart. How's that for metaphor? Nothing like the real thing.

He chewed on my shoulder, working through the muscle like a dog chewing gristle. I kneed him in the groin and shoved him off me; a chunk of my shoulder remained in his mouth like a meatball.

More zombies streamed in. Lucy fought them off with our Peruvian rain stick, the annoying rain sound harmonizing with the living dead's moans until the stick broke and dried beans spilled onto the hardwood floor. Lucy grabbed my elbow and pulled me down to the basement, where we were safe, at least temporarily. There was only one entrance, through the kitchen. We locked the deadbolt behind us, dragged flattened cardboard boxes up the stairs, and duct-taped them over the doorway.

It was classic victim behavior, actually, seen in dozens of horror movies: Grab whatever you can, stupid humans, and throw it at the door. Hell, use a solid granite tombstone if you've got it. Doesn't matter. If you lock yourself in a room, eventually the monsters will get in.

Lucy and I huddled between a giant plastic Santa and the LL Bean tent we used just once—and then in the backyard. Now we'd never go to Yosemite.

"What should I do?" I asked her, gripping my shoulder.

"What are your options?"

"As I see it, suicide or zombification."

"Don't focus on the negative, Jack. Think! How can we fix this?"

I made my jaw go slack and drooled. "Brains. I could eat your brains!" I held out my arms like Boris Karloff in *Frankenstein,* a film that disgraces monsters everywhere.

In Mary Shelley's original novel, the creature is sympathetic, a victim of human hatred and intolerance; he speaks French, reads Milton, and loves flowers. He is not a natural-born killer; society turns him into one.

Karloff's mute brute, on the other hand, yearns for flesh and blood from the get-go. He turns crowds into mobs and creates fear and loathing, yet his version is the one that lives in our imagination, not Shelley's.

To pervert Rodney Dangerfield: Monsters can't get no respect.

Lucy slapped my forearm. "That's not funny," she said, and started to cry.

"You cry because there's truth in my jest," I said. "Which is the goal of all effective humor, exposing the hidden pain in pleasure. The sorrow underneath all we do. The tragedy of our lives. I will be one of them soon, my dear, and I may indeed want to eat your brains. I have a decision to make. To be dead or undead. That is the question."

"Let me look at your shoulder."

The area surrounding the bite was plum purple and gashed open, the blood already coagulated. I felt beatific, angelic, but my failure to bleed was no miracle; it was the virus congealing my blood, freezing it, stopping it in its tracks and turning me into something both sub- and über-human. If the news reports and movies were true, I would have flulike symptoms—a fever, vomiting, chills, joint pain—then a numbing sensation, followed by a brief death culminating in my reanimation as one of the living dead. The whole process could take anywhere from six to thirty-six hours—the length of the average birth.

Lucy glanced at the wound and moved several inches away from me. "You could try electrocuting yourself with the Christmas tree lights," she suggested.

"Why don't we have any tools?" I asked, getting up to poke around the basement. "I can't even find a hammer. Didn't we ever have occasion to hammer something? A nail perhaps?"

I was already speaking in the past tense.

"A hammer would come in handy now," Lucy said. "We could fortify the door."

"Or rope," I said. "Why don't we have any rope? We don't even have a rope to hang yourself with."

"Or a pot to piss in."

"Rope wouldn't do anything anyway. I have to destroy my brain. With hanging I'd just be a zombie with a broken neck. That could prove to be a disadvantage in my search for food, I suppose."

"But does natural selection, survival of the fittest, apply to the living dead?" Lucy asked. "I mean, does it matter at that point? Will you need to compete with other zombies for food? Or will you live, or unlive, regardless?"

My bite site stank like rotten pork shoulder. My flesh was putrefying and I felt feverish. Or maybe it was psychosomatic. I sat down on the concrete floor and looked at my wife.

"It's a valid question," she said, "if you decide to, you know, go the zombie route."

Lucy wore her hair in a short, mannish cut, which I wished she would grow out into a softer style. But I never asked her to. God forbid I should appear controlling or, even worse, a card-carrying member of the patriarchy who dared suggest she assume a more traditionally feminine appearance.

She was a big-boned woman, but thin, so that her knees, elbows, and feet stuck out like knobs, almost bursting through her pale, blue-veined skin. She could have gained fifteen pounds. I could see her skeleton, the thinnest veneer of flesh covering it, with no body fat to speak of. Although I loved her dearly, sometimes, in bed, her bones ground into me and hurt.

But yum. If I could gnaw on one of those bones now as I write this. Just a strip of flesh hanging down would do. The smallest sinew is all I need.

MUFFLED BY THE cellar door, the moans of the undead sounded like an avant-garde chorus, a John Cage composition. *The United States of the Undead: A Sonata in the Key of Reanimation.* At the end of the cacophonous piece, the orchestra, consisting of infected musicians in tattered tuxedos, eats the audience.

It was hot; my shoulder was disintegrating. Lucy held my forehead and stroked my back while I vomited everything I'd ever ingested: Hershey's Kisses, funnel cakes, peach pits, mother's milk.

"You're a regular Florence Nightingale," I told her, wiping my lips with the back of my hand. There was a metallic taste in my mouth, like I was sucking on rusty nails or had eaten liver at a roadside diner in the rural South.

"I'd rather be Hot Lips Houlihan," she said.

"Walt Whitman was a nurse in the Civil War."

"I wonder what Walt would've thought of the living dead," Lucy said.

"He'd drink the tasteless water of their souls."

Lucy felt my forehead. She fought back tears, my little trouper.

"You're burning up," she said.

"I'm on fire for you, baby. You make me hot."

She kissed my cheek. "Let's make love," she whispered. "One last time."

Her voice was atonal and shrill, a screech owl in my ear, Yoko Ono singing. I knew it was just my senses, heightened by the fever, as well as the virus coursing through my veins, but I needed her to be quiet.

So I kissed her. She sucked in her breath and turned her head, wrinkling her nose and gagging. I must have tasted like death, but still she bent forward for another kiss.

"You need an Altoid," she said.

"They're curiously strong," I said, "and I'm decaying."

I took her in my arms and we kissed again. A violent chill overtook me and I turned my head to the side, coughing up what looked like a piece of lung.

"What I wouldn't give for a cigarette," I said.

"This would be an excellent time for you to start smoking. I mean, why not? At this point, you've got nothing to lose."

She put her head on my shoulder, then started back in horror when she felt its wetness. A few pieces of my meat stuck to her hair. They were the size and color of bacon bits and although they were pulsating, throbbing, beating with my heart, I couldn't feel a thing.

Lucy stood up, located the stuff sack for our tent, and tied it around my wound in a sloppy tourniquet.

"What's the plan?" she asked.

"Plan?"

"Come on, Jack. You always have a plan. And I always think it won't work and doubt you and beg you not to do it. You ignore me and do it anyway and it does work, wonderfully, in fact, and everything's okay and I'm proved wrong again."

"Like the time I successfully lobbied to deny Dobson tenure?"

"I was thinking of that ugly-ass cat-scratching post you constructed out of old carpet and clothes. But yeah, poor Dobson. I felt sorrier for his wife, actually."

"He's an idiot"—I coughed up a speck of blood—"and she's a bitch."

"They're probably zombies by now."

"And the cats loved that post. They used it all the time, sparing the ridiculously expensive couch you made us buy."

"My point precisely. You were absolutely right. You always are."

The undead rattled the door. They wouldn't leave until they broke it down; they had nothing better to do.

"I don't have a plan, Lucy-kins," I said. "Unfortunately, there is no master plan. No meta-narrative."

"No clockmaker?"

"No exit."

"Hell is other zombies," she said.

"Hell is for children."

"Love is a battlefield."

"A 'Battle Hymn of the Republic,'" I said. "Cowritten by Plato and Jesse Jackson. Break beats provided by Chuck D."

Lucy put her chin on her knees and wrapped her arms around her shins. "I can't do this," she said to the floor.

"Can't do what?"

"We've got a real problem here, Jack," she whispered. Her eyes had a surprised look about them, round and alert, the eyebrows high on her forehead and plucked to a thin arch. "In a few hours, you're going to be a zombie. And I'm either going to be devoured by you or else bitten and turned into a zombie myself. At the very least I'll be a widow." She paused and cocked her head to one side. "But if you join the ranks of the undead," she continued, placing a finger on her lips, "and I manage to escape unharmed and survive as a human, would I be a widow then? Technically speaking, I mean. Is there a word yet for that relationship?"

"Hmmm, it's thorny. I couldn't say. Language doesn't evolve that quickly. Or does it? These are the most extenuating of circumstances and I'm sure future cunning linguists will have a field day with the zombie-related lexicon, orthography, neologisms, what have you."

A rat scurried in the corner. Death kept knocking on the door.

Every child's fear of the dark is justified. There is a monster hiding under your bed.

In our collective imagination, the babysitter's phone rings: "Get out!" we yell at her. "He's in the house!"

"The best option," I continued, "is to kill myself before I die, or you could kill me, whichever, so you could escape."

"How?"

"Slit my wrists, maybe. There's got to be a sharp implement around here somewhere. Or you could run the rake over my face. Then use me as a shield. Hold me in front of you, if I'm not too heavy. Conjure your superhuman strength. Pretend you're a mother lifting a Volkswagen off her kids. The zombies will fall upon me in an eating frenzy and you run, Lucy, you run to the hills. Run for your life."

"You're forgetting about your brain," Lucy said. "We have to destroy your brain or else you'll just be a half-eaten zombie. Unless they eat all of you and you disappear. Poof. No more Jack."

"Plus, I'm not quite sure I want to die." I lay down. I couldn't feel my extremities and I'd never been hotter. I took off my glasses and pressed my cheek to the cool concrete. The door was holding, but barely. Zombies would be in our sanctuary soon—either me or the ones at the top of the stairs.

"What if being undead is better than death itself?" I asked, and closed my eyes.

That's the last thing I remember of my human life. Resting my head on the soothing concrete, Lucy's hand stroking my hair. The ground smelled like dirt, must, mold, and gasoline. I smelled like Beethoven decomposing.

"Don't eat me, Jack," Lucy said from a great distance. "Don't you dare eat me."

CHAPTER TWO

OH, THE HUNGER. So hungry. Waking up, my body was in flames. A human torch. A burning man. The all-consuming fires of hell. As in Dante's *Inferno*. As in eternal damnation. You can stop, drop, and roll all you want, there's no putting out this blaze.

Cognitive function was minimal. At first. Brain turning to mashed potatoes. Body falling to pieces . . . leprous leprosy. Leper, I was. Leper, I still am.

Upstairs, a noise. Some part of my mind registered: dog. Fluffy. Must go, stumble, waddle, traipse like the Mummy, follow the whimper. I stopped in our conjugal bathroom and stared at my reflection. Jonesing for flesh, manic for meat, I scribbled letters on the mirror with my finger. Inscription, graphomania. The first hint of my sentience.

This is what I wrote: *Brains!*

Fluffy was Lucy's dog. A damn toy poodle. I ate her. She was very funny. I mean furry. Why did I write funny? Furry. Or fury. I ate her in a funny furry fury. There was little meat on Fluffy. Tiny brain. The fluffy white fur of Fluffy fell on the bedroom carpet and I learned: In a pinch, any meat will suffice.

When empty, my stomach is a pit of burning coals; every muscle is tearing apart and my tendons are eaten by wolves, my liver chewed up like the liver of Prometheus.

The needle and the damage done.

Dear God, where was my Lucy?

I walked outside and stood at the end of the driveway. Our modest suburban street had been transformed into a Japanese monster movie. Humans ran like B-movie extras, like people running from an alien attack or a blitzkrieg, looking over their shoulders at Armageddon.

Cars screeched out of driveways and smashed into telephone poles and each other, going nowhere. Grandmas and children were left trapped inside SUVs and minivans, staring at the disaster through the windows like they were on a drive-thru safari, looking for the lions.

And chasing them all, the cause of their terror: me.

The old lady from next door ran by in her house slippers. In one hand she wielded a spatula, in the other kitchen shears. "Jack!" she cried when she saw me. "Not you too!"

Lucy and I had hated the biddy. She was the kind of anal-retentive shrew who brought out the leaf blower for one lousy leaf. Once, when Fluffy accidentally crapped in her yard, she picked up his poo and threw it over the fence like a monkey at the zoo.

I grabbed her wrinkly elbow and bit into her arm. She hit me over the head with the spatula as if I were a pancake she wanted to flatten. I didn't even flinch.

Another zombie moved in and bit the back of her neck, then another and another, until she was surrounded. I stepped away from the group; the old bitch's arms were over her head like someone bobbing in deep water. Not waving, but drowning. Her utensils fell to the ground.

A young mother ran toward me, clutching her baby to her breast. Every evening as Lucy and I sat on the couch watching Brian Williams, this woman power-walked past our picture window. We didn't know her name or which house she lived in, but she'd become a fixture in our lives, as reliable as the evening news and David Letterman.

I reached out and snatched the baby from her as she powered by; Mama fell to her knees.

"Please," she pleaded. "Not the baby."

Oh, the melodrama. I clutched the baby by its arms, shaking it. I bared my teeth, drooling like Grendel over a virgin sacrifice.

"Mooooaaah!" I roared.

The baby's face was scrunched up, its eyes squeezed shut. It was utterly helpless. Defenseless. Fay Wray in the arms of King Kong, as tender and juicy as veal.

The need to feed grew within me. It was monumental, rivaling the needs of Michael Jackson, Adolf Hitler, Barbra Streisand, Henry VIII, and King Tut . . . combined. I was a practical joke played by Mother Nature.

Can a being with infinite desire ever be sated?

I opened my mouth as wide as I could, a circus geek with his chicken, Ozzy Osbourne with his bat.

"No!" Mama sobbed and plunged a knitting needle into my forearm.

The needle stuck out like I was a voodoo doll. I dropped the infant and Mama scooped her child up and cradled it. Baby pulled at Mother's shirt, exposing a milky expanse of swollen breast. I understood its hunger. Mama turned tail and took off, dodging zombies like a running back, baby tucked under her arm like a football.

I pulled the needle out and walked toward the house. Behind me, I heard screams and moans, teeth crunching bones. The sounds of civilization coming to an end.

ZOMBIES DON'T SLEEP. I wandered the house looking for Lucy, half afraid I would find her and eat her, more afraid I already had. I left messages for her in the furniture's dust, scrawled a letter on the dry-erase board in the kitchen, stuck Post-it notes on the walls of our bedroom. They all said the same thing: *Forgive me, Lucy, for being a monster.*

I might have spent hours or days walking from room to room. I couldn't tell anymore. Time meant nothing. The past and the future no longer existed. The present was the only thing that felt real.

How Buddhist of me . . . if Buddhists ate babies for brunch.

When I gazed at myself in the antique gilt mirror over the fireplace, "I started back," as Frankenstein's monster said, "unable to believe that it was indeed I who was reflected in the mirror; and when I became fully convinced that I was in reality the monster that I am, I was filled with the bitterest sensations of despondence and mortification."

My hair was matted and dreadlocked. In life the look would have been trendy for a certain demographic; even the clots of blood and chunks of meat and bone embedded in the tangle could have passed for over-the-top Goth. I had the pallor of the undead—pale as the kitchen sink. My wrinkles, lines around my eyes and mouth that once connoted a life fully lived, were etched in black and red, a caricature of distinguished age. My once gym-toned and muscled body was wasting and my shoulder, the site of my bite, was falling off like spit-roasted barbecue. Yet I felt no pain.

I pressed my nose against the mirror. No fog. No breath.

On the mantel was a framed photo of Lucy smearing cake on my face. It's a scene replayed at a million wedding receptions: The bride shoving frosting at the groom, intentionally missing his mouth, her own mouth opened wide with laughter. The ritual is simultaneously playful and sadistic, combining food and sex, dominance and submission, consumption and power. Sugar, spice, and everything nice.

I swept my hand across the mantel, sending the photo, a ceramic vase, and a brass cat flying. I felt dramatic and romantic: a soap opera hero, Hamlet wringing his hands, lonely Adam pining for Eve.

There was no use rambling around in that house of memories. Like Lucy said, I always have a plan. A purpose.

Professor Jack Barnes was taking a trip, a pilgrimage, in search of others like him. I couldn't be the only corpse with consciousness, the only brain-eater with a brain. I wasn't entirely alone. Was I?

I REJOINED MY fellow zombies in the street, following the herd, moaning as they did, lifting my arms as I walked, stiff as a board. Admittedly, my gait was a bit more strident, more competent than the others'. I had cognition on my side and I was a relatively young zombie; most of my body parts were intact.

Car alarms blared; sirens wailed; and my shoulder tingled. I sensed humans nearby but saw none. They were hiding in basements, no doubt, cowering in bathtubs or eating canned spinach in bomb shelters. A helicopter flew overhead, spraying us with machine-gun fire, but the attack was short and perfunctory, the equivalent of a drive-by shooting. The chopper was headed south, probably to Saint Louis to save the Arch. No one cared about our tiny town and its corn, cows, and liberal arts college.

I searched the eyes of my companions as we shuffled along, looking for a glimmer of intelligence, recognition, memory. I saw nothing. Their eyes were soulless and flat, devoid of thought, empty of feeling, and hell-bent on finding loved ones and neighbors to eat. Instinct alone propelled them forward, one rank foot in front of the other. Programmed for one thing and one thing only, they wouldn't stop until they got it.

Marie Delaney from across the street fell in beside me. In life she had been a doctor, and a generous one at that; one evening when Lucy refused to go to the hospital after punching the wall of the sunroom in a fit of jealous rage, we'd knocked on Marie's door. After a brief examination, the good doctor prepared an ice pack for Lucy's hand—no questions asked and no payment accepted.

Lucy's anger had been justified. She'd discovered a transgression of mine, an affair of no consequence with a graduate student, a dim meaty woman with breasts the size of a newborn's head, both of which, breast and metaphorical infant, I'd gladly eat now. That would be more pleasant than screwing the woman was, come to think of it.

Zombie Marie still had on her scrubs. They were splattered with blood, a Jackson Pollock of red and black and forest green. Her neck was broken; it lolled on her left shoulder, causing her to walk in a lopsided fashion. The classic zombie shuffle.

I tried to speak with her, to ask if she had a destination, a plan, a leader, but to my dismay, instead of a well-formed sentence loaded with the requisite layers of meaning—Do you like me? Remember that night we went skinny-dipping in the Smiths' pool? Thank you for examining Lucy—inarticulate moans came from my gash of a mouth.

A caveman, I was preverbal. A boy raised by wolves. Helen Keller before her education. Nothing more than an animal.

Marie looked at me and her eyes flickered in recognition. For a microflash, a nanosecond, she grasped our predicament. Her eyes cleared to chestnut brown and I saw understanding in their depths. Grief beyond repair. Then the milky-white film, thick as cataracts, returned to her irises, and the pathos was gone.

If eyes are windows to the soul, then Marie's soul had left the building.

We wandered en masse. There were no sidewalks in our town. Before zombification, cars ruled the streets. Now, we creatures commanded them. We passed a brick home guarded by a concrete goose lawn ornament wearing an Uncle Sam suit for the Fourth of July, then another brick home with concrete deer grazing on the lawn, and a third brick home flying the American flag. We hit the highway and passed the Wal-Mart. The parking lot was almost empty.

Zombies communicate as insects do, through pheromones or memes or telepathy. We moved as one past the store; no one broke off from the group to search the supercenter. The building was deserted, although I now know that Wal-Mart can be an excellent place to hunt. Humans raid the store for food and supplies; we raid the store for humans. Big fish follows small fish follows zooplankton follows phytoplankton. Your basic food chain. Ninth-grade biology.

Wal-Mart—their people make the difference . . . and the evening meal.

At the edge of town we turned onto a gravel road as if guided by an unseen hand. Cows munching on grass watched us as we filed by, a writhing stinking mass of the undead. They were undisturbed by our moaning. A few even lowed back.

The road ended and we stumbled up against a barbed-wire fence fortified with an eight-foot wall made of car tires and hubcaps, car doors and grilles. To the right was the Chariton River, to the left a field of soy; behind the fortress was A. J. Riley's junkyard and within, the siren call that lured us: the unmistakable scent of human flesh.

Hyenas let loose on gazelles. Termites on wood. Maggots on meat. Fleas on rats. Amoebas on fleas on rats. We swarmed the wall.

It was a slo-mo frenzy. Rubber and steel fell as we climbed the structure in our shambling way, taking our time, like slippered old men shuffling down hospital hallways. A few zombies fell off the wall and onto the fence, speared like martini olives.

I was the first to reach the top. I hoisted myself over and tumbled down the other side, landing on my feet. A Rottweiler ran at me, a one-headed Cerberus guarding the gates of hell, and sank his teeth into my ankle. I shook him off as if he were a kitten, slamming his body into the wall just as Marie hit the ground. She jumped him. I heard his high-pitched whimper as she tore into his muscular neck.

There was a building in front of me and a Honda Civic to my right, its hood missing and its engine covered with rust. Behind the building were the junked cars, each one as decrepit and dead as we were, each roof a tombstone.

Inside the office, there was a gunshot. Blood splattered on the window in a Rorschach pattern of a dove in flight. I headed for it, a phalanx of zombies trailing behind me, clustered together like a zygote. By the time I made it through the door, most of A. J. Riley's brains had seeped out of the hole he'd blasted through his head. I got down on my hands and knees and sucked them up like an aardvark sucking ants.

Brian Williams was on the television mounted near the ceiling, his voice calm and professional. "We are coming to you live from our studios in Chicago," he said, "Ground Zero of this horrific outbreak, where Dr. Howard Stein, the scientist responsible for the virus, lives and works. Sources reveal Stein is working with government officials on a cure or a mutation, pursuing any avenue that might slow the spreading, control the infected, and spare precious lives. In the meantime, you are advised to stay indoors and avoid contact with anyone who has been bitten . . ."

I was listening to Brian's report and stuffing my maw when the zombie cluster caught up with me a few minutes later. I stood up and waved my arms, yelling, "Moaaaggh!"

The masses stopped; they bumped into each other like kindergarteners forming a line for candy. "Moaaaggh!" I repeated, and stepped aside to let the mindless demons feed.

CHAPTER THREE

I HAVEN'T SHAT since my transformation. The phenomenology of feces. How come I haven't expelled the flesh I've eaten? What kind of chemical reaction takes place within me? How is it I extract strength from the meat I eat? I become skinnier, rottener, deader, by the hour.

After eating A. J., I headed to Chicago to look for Howard Stein. Like the Oracle at Delphi, Stein would answer my questions, prophesy my future, provide valuable information. He might even be aware of my condition. Any decent scientist would have planned for the contingency, perhaps even hoped for it. Any decent creator would love and protect his best creation.

In my tweed jacket pocket, I carried the tools necessary to record what I could: my pen and notebook. What more did I need? Posterity would thank me.

As I passed the university, I joined the zombies wandering around the quad, aimless as human students waiting for Intro to World Religions to begin. I stumbled through the fountain and walked over the rosebushes, not even feeling the thorns. I was shuffling, favoring my bitten shoulder, the arm attached to it hanging limp, the stuff-sack tourniquet long gone.

All at once I smelled it, wafting on a warm breeze. My shoulder sang with it. Sweet as summer corn. Sweeter than Lucy's sweet-scented snatch. The sweet sweet smell of human flesh.

The student zombies smelled it too. Every undead head perked up and we moved as one toward the fragrance.

Oh, he was easy to find. Silly human. He'd barricaded himself in his office; a gray metal filing cabinet containing twenty-five years of teacher evaluations blocked our entrance. A group of us pawed at the door until it opened; the filing cabinet toppled and reams of useless paper covered the floor.

Professor Barnes made me cry, one student had written.

This class was a waste of time, opined another.

I knew the human: Dr. Ernst Welk, chair of the English department, hair white as snow, belly like Santa Claus. He could have easily evaded and outrun us—we move as if through sludge—but he panicked. The scene was a parody of every clichéd horror movie from *White Zombie* to *Friday the 13th Part Million: Geriatric Jason.* The slow but relentless killer walks without a care in the world, confident he'll get his prey if he simply stays the course. And the stupid victim, looking back as she runs, trips over a tree limb or her own high heels.

I felt a line of monsters behind me as I advanced on Dr. Welk. My ancestors: Count Dracula, the Wolfman, Jason Voorhees, Michael Myers, Freddy Krueger, the Red Death in his mask and vestments. Every party has a pooper; that's why we invited the Boogeyman.

Ernst ran out of the office and made it halfway down the hall before he tripped and fell over a chair, the kind with the attached desk. He was wearing a suit and tie. He must be crazy, I thought. Why is he here? And in those clothes? Did he return for some document or has he been here from the start? And just how long has that been?

I was the first ghoul to reach him. The others were slower, a good twenty feet behind me.

"Barnes," he said, "can you hear me? Are you in there?"

"Mmmpph," I said. "Uuuhhhh!"

Heaven forgive me, but I wanted him. Bad. I was a nymphomaniac for his hot flesh. He was portly and succulent, lying there on the circa-1970s purple carpet with his hands in front of his face like a gay pinup from the golden age of porn.

"Jack," he began, "about your sabbatical . . ."

I ached; my soul ached. I was junk-sick and hungry for booze, pills, McDonald's, sex, cars, chewing gum, crank, crack, Diet Coke, laudanum, Internet porn, video games—all of it. Take every weak human addiction and multiply it by the living, the dead, and the living dead, from George Washington to Saddam Hussein, from Homer to Bono, and that might come close to describing the magnitude of my hunger.

I desired, very much, to eat him.

"You deserved a semester off," he said. "I'm sorry."

Ernst was flat on his back like an overturned beetle. One of his stubby legs was twisted around the chrome leg of the chair; the desk was poking him in the rib cage. He struggled to free himself, but every time he reached down to pull on his thigh, the desk dug deeper into his side. The man was weak from a lifetime of sitting; his arms were roly-poly, with no visible biceps, triceps, or delts. His suit was wrinkled and stained. He had been a competent adminis-trator, and that's not saying much.

"Damn it, Jack," he said, trying to drag both his body and the desk away from me and wincing from the pain. "Have you no hu-manity left?"

I got down on my hands and knees next to him: my boss, my colleague, my savior, my lamb. Appeaser of the beast in me. I took a bite. The memory is as clear as Wordsworth's claim for poetry: emotion recollected in tranquility.

I started with his stomach and received a mouthful of poly-cotton blend. I spit it out and with the next bite hit pay dirt. His skin tasted like baby powder and musk. There was a thick layer of fat surrounding the muscle; it was gristly and responded to the teeth with an al dente spring. I heard the pack gathering behind me, moaning for stink. Ernst raised himself on one elbow, screamed, and kicked his leg like a toddler throwing a tantrum.

"You always were an asshole," he said.

Tell me something I don't know. Meal ticket.

IN THE MIDDLE of Iowa I was chased by a group of men in orange vests and waders. I was running through the corn, Ernst's broken femur jammed in the back pocket of my Dockers.

There were zombie hunters everywhere. Shotgun-wielding rednecks who aimed for the head.

"There's one now!" a man yelled.

"Holy shit," said another. "That one's running."

"Impossible. The shits don't know how to run."

"Sure looks like he's running."

Someone laughed. "You call that running, Bobby? Now I know why you wasn't much of a ball player in school. The thing's legs are barely lifting off the ground. He's a shuffler, all right. Running. Shit, them things can't run."

"I think Bobby's right, sheriff. Whether or not he's got the skill, he's got the will. Looks like he's trying to get away from us."

I didn't stop moving.

"Damnedest thing," the sheriff said. "He does appear to have a plan."

The sheriff gave me too much credit; I didn't have a plan. I had one thought: Survive. And that meant protecting my brain.

Since I was—and am—a corpse, a fleeing, decaying corpse, I leave body parts behind when I run through vegetation. Little chunks of falling-off flesh cling to tall grass, raspberry vines, or brambles, making me easy to track.

I felt a stinging in my back and lurched forward.

"Got 'im!"

"You slowed him down, son, but you don't have him, not 'til you hit him in the head and he's flat on the ground."

"Just take your time and aim, Bobby. He ain't going nowhere in a hurry."

I felt another sting at the site of my neighbor's bite. I fell down and moaned.

"That time I got 'im for sure."

"Don't get cocky. It's best to check your kill, make sure it's dead. Just like you do with a deer."

"Did you hear him though?"

"Sounded damn-near human."

"I don't like this one. Gives me the creeps."

"More creeps than the others? You are a piece of work, Bobby. Grow some balls, why dontcha? Now go finish the job. Put that stench down for good."

I crawled away, elbow over elbow, and hid in a stand of corn. I took out the only weapons I had: my notebook and pen.

Help me, Bobby, I wrote. *Spare me.*

The letters were shaky and the pen strokes thin; it looked like it was written by a child.

Bobby rustled through the stalks.

"Hurry up," his comrades yelled. "There's another group on the horizon."

With my head down, not daring to look young Bobby in the eye for fear I'd attack, I held up the paper.

"Holy shit," Bobby said. "What are you?"

Gunshots rang out from another part of the field.

"Bobby!" they called. "What's going on?"

I cradled my head in my arms, protecting it, supplicating before this farm boy. Bobby shot the ground next to me.

"Got 'im!" he yelled as he ran off.

Thank you, Bobby, child of the corn. I owe you my life.

THE HIGHWAY WAS littered with abandoned vehicles. A traffic jam without road ragers shouting into cell phones. The grass was yellow and brown, scorched by the sun. The crops were dry and neglected.

For breakfast I veered into the trees and found a rabbit's nest. The mother and her five bunnies screamed as I bit into them. The sound was unexpected, as piercing and angry as the cry of a newborn stuffed in a trash can at prom. The rabbits' brains were small, their intestines filled with hard pellets like Skittles. I stored a foot in my pocket for luck.

Still hungry, I shuffled back to the highway.

The dead walked with me, wobbling like newly birthed calves, bumper-car zombies going nowhere. The ratio, Blake called it. Hamster wheels within hamster wheels.

The bullet holes in my back, the bite on my shoulder . . . it occurred to me that if I stopped the decay, I could escape the grave, live forever.

A Hummer drove down the highway, tearing through the zombie throng like Moses parting a Red Sea of bloody corpses.

The driver barely slowed down; he knocked over the walking dead as if they were bowling pins and he was going for a perfect game. I stepped out of the way and called out to the others to do the same.

"Mmoohhhaaa. Oooaaahhh!" I cried. Pathetic. My lips barely parted and my mouth felt like a crawfish castle—dry and full of mud. I was stuck in a body that would not obey me. A stroke victim, I was locked in. A rotting portable prison.

A walking putrefying metaphor.

I, Robot.

I, Zombie.

And, oh, those silly zombies. Letting themselves be run over like skunks and possum. And then worse, picking themselves back up afterward, maimed but mobile. Resurrected roadkill. The tenacity of the undead. Their blind stupidity. A teenage zombette still wearing her soccer uniform, her legs were crushed by the Hummer's tires. That didn't stop her, however. She sprang back up like one of the Hydra's heads and continued forward on those flattened legs, her red braids and braces gleaming. She was damn near perky.

As the vehicle passed me, I peered into the windows. Inside was a nuclear family—mom, dad, two girls, and a boy. Even a dog—some kind of terrier yapping away, its nose and paws pressed against the glass. The mother, a ponytailed blonde in a pink yoga outfit, stared back at me. We made eye contact and I flashed her the peace sign and grinned, dislodging a clump of crust in the corner of my mouth. The woman put her hand to her throat and in that instant, I felt known. Understood. My sentience was acknowledged by another thinking being. And then they were gone, hightailing it down the highway, crashing into parked cars and catatonic zombies.

I was even lonelier after that brief connection. Like Orestes or Princess Di, I was chased by demons both real and imagined. I needed a companion. I'd have taken Lilith if Eve was unavailable, but I preferred Eve. More compliant, made from my rib. Except for that apple thing, Eve would be perfect.

THE DEAD WALK at a snail's pace, complete with trails of slime. At the rate I was going, I'd decompose before reaching Chicago and finding Stein. A pickup truck cruised down the road, picking off members of the horde at random. When it stopped, the driver bending down to retrieve something from the floor—a plug of chaw, no doubt—and his passenger reloading, I acted.

Climbing in was an effort. My joints were stiff with rigor mortis. I lay down between a spare tire and a tool case. Empty beer cans and shotgun shells rattled around me and a gun rack loomed above. I covered myself with a blue tarp.

In life, I wouldn't have looked twice at these men. They were large and one wore an oversized T-shirt advertising Pepsi. Both had on NASCAR ball caps.

The only Homer they knew was Simpson; their favorite beer was Bud Light. Their idea of an art film was *The Shawshank Redemption* and their wives collected Precious Moments figurines. What could I possibly talk about with them? The weather?

It was all I could do not to eat them.

"That one over there is almost pretty," one said.

"Shoot her!"

"Now hold on a minute. She looks recently turned—probably still warm inside there. Fresh."

"You ain't never tried that, have you?"

"Screwing a zombie? Hell no!"

"But you've thought about it?"

"It's crossed my mind. I suppose you'd have to tie her up first and gag her, or cover her whole head with something to protect yourself. Like a Wal-Mart bag maybe. Or a catcher's mask. Then I guess you could just do it regular."

"You are one sick fuck, Earl."

"On second thought, doggy-style might be the safest bet."

"I'm gonna pretend I didn't hear that."

There was a shotgun blast.

"Got her!" Earl said.

"Good shot. Right in the head."

"Kind of seems like a waste though."

"She did look like your wife." He laughed.

"That ain't funny. My wife *is* one of 'em."

Poor man. The title of his life's movie? *I Married a Zombie Bitch*.

The men rolled up their windows and the truck picked up speed. Hidden under my tarp, I exercised self-control. Mindful restraint.

Denying my instincts, displaying the discipline of an ascetic monk, I took out my affirmation journal.

This is what I wrote:

A To-Not-Do List

1. Do not smash the back window and attack the driver.
2. Do not climb on top of the cab and slap your bloody hand on the windshield.
3. Do not press your face against the glass and bare your teeth at Earl.
4. Do not eat the rednecks.

Oh, but their dull stupid brains. I reckon they're tasty.

WE DROVE ALL night through the cornfields of the Midwest. Lying on my back, I peeked out of the tarp and up at the stars. Amazingly, they were still there.

I may have prayed. If I believed in God I would have, but I was raised an atheist.

"God was wounded during World War One," my father taught me, "and died in the gas chambers of the Holocaust. Don't believe any of that supernatural mumbo-jumbo."

My paternal grandparents were wealthy Jewish doctors who fled the Nazis in 1937. My grandmother was the first woman to graduate from the University of Vienna. When they arrived in America, they had a strongbox full of diamonds and identification papers. They had money tucked away in a Swiss bank account. And they had their lives and their children by the hand.

They left their drapes and Turkish rugs, pots and pans, real estate and religion to the Nazis. For all I know, Hitler himself slept in their oak four-poster bed underneath the feather duvet and on top of the dozens of pillows Oma kept fluffed and spotless. Oma and Opa never went back to Vienna, but Oma often talked about what they left behind.

Her stories ended the same way every time: "And that, *kleine* Jack, is how the Boorsteins became the Barneses."

I have Viennese property I could claim. There's an apartment building and a house. A pea patch and some vacant lots. Lucy begged me to take her to my ancestral home for our honeymoon, but I refused.

"Too painful?" she asked.

"Too boring," I lied.

We honeymooned in the Caribbean instead, where Lucy wore a bikini and ran into the ocean, her heels almost touching the crescent moons of her bottom. She looked over her shoulder at me and I chased after her, grabbing her by the waist and kissing her; she was meatier then and I adored her.

"Float like you're dead," she'd said, treading water.

I rolled face-first into the sea, my arms splayed out, my legs hanging straight down. Lucy jumped on, straddling me piggyback style.

I dove underwater then, sunken with the weight of my wife. I could hear her giggling above me and I swam as hard as I could, breaking the surface like a dolphin, Lucy riding me like a nymph.

If only Lucy were with me as the truck bounced along. She would have made a child's game out of our concealment. Hide and Seek or Kick the Can.

Lightning flashed and it started to rain. I pulled the tarp over my head, my fingers leaving behind a thick coat of crud, sticky as glue.

Fat raindrops hit the tarp; each one sounded like a nail pounding me deeper into my coffin.

CHAPTER FOUR

THE TRUCK STOPPED at a TA Travel Center in the middle of that godforsaken, corn-infested state. It was morning, the sky was clear, and the area appeared to be free of zombies. Humans milled about, filling up their gas tanks, gathering food and drink, exchanging information and gossip. No money changed hands, indicating a massive breakdown in the economy as well as society as a whole. Nothing is more integral to America than the accumulation of wealth. And if no one paid for anything, no one made a profit.

In the wake of the Zombie Apocalypse, humanity had gone commie. Zombie Joe McCarthy must be scratching at the walls of his crypt.

As soon as Earl and the driver went inside the truck stop, I peered over the top of the bed. Seeing no one in the immediate vicinity, I climbed out.

My stomach was a vast and empty black hole.

I lumbered from car to car, hiding behind wheels and trunks, pretending to be an injured soldier in a Vietnam War movie. Charlie got my shoulder, I radioed in. Turned it into pork for his stir-fry.

I watched the humans through the windows of the truck stop. Clustered in groups, dispensing soda from the fountain, unwrapping Snickers bars, leafing through *Field and Stream*. The women fondled molded plastic angels, slipping them into their purses.

More for protection than decoration, I imagined. Oh, Archangel Michael, made in China, save me from the vampiric undead; end this eternal waking nightmare.

Inside the curly heads of those ladies were their brains: beautiful, bountiful, bubbly, bewitching, bedazzling brains.

I was thirteen years old again, beholding my first pair of boobs, only this longing was beyond sexual. Swelling to godlike proportions, my desire eclipsed the sun.

I shuffled past a white El Dorado tucked in the far side of the lot and my shoulder tingled. There was movement in the front seat. I looked in and there she sat, a young woman no more than twenty-five, staring back at me with eyes so large and full of fright the irises had disappeared.

What she was doing in the parking lot alone, I'll never know. Nor do I care.

I tried the handle. Locked. She scrunched down in her seat and put her hands over her head. Not a fighter, this one. More like an ostrich. I wondered where her protector was. Undoubtedly she had one, a pretty woman like her.

I used to look at women and see hips and ass, hair and snatch. How pedestrian that seems now. Leave procreation to the living. I'll take gray matter.

Then I thought: Don't eat the whole thing, Jack. Bite her, just enough for a snack. Quell the riotous beast within, infect her with the virus, and take her for your mate. Your Eve.

She was pale, alabaster even, with short dark hair cut into Louise Brooks bangs. I pointed at her and she put her hand over her mouth. With her wide, terrified eyes and the French tips on her nails, she looked like a 1950s scream queen.

I scanned the area for a weapon and located a tire iron. What else? So far, my postlife had been cinematic, a travesty of a zombie movie, with the literary addition of a tragic and self-conscious hero, a misunderstood creature with which to sympathize. Of course there'd be a handy weapon to help him!

And don't feel guilty for your empathy. You're supposed to identify with me, causing you to question what it means to be human and moral—and to be grateful for your own miserable lot in life. So go ahead and sympathize. Construct me as the "other."

Let me be your monster.

I grabbed the tire iron with both hands, climbed onto the hood of the car, and raised the tool over my head. At the pinnacle of the arc, the muscles in my rotten shoulder shifted, a chunk of meat detached, and my grip slipped. I tottered. Human voices drifted from around the corner. Eve stared at me, her expression a mixture of terror and fascination, attraction and repulsion. She looked, above all else, curious. As for me, I felt sublime.

I brought the tire iron down and the windshield buckled and cracked in such a way that I was able to rip it out in one piece. I had no idea that was how windshields were constructed. I expected something much more theatrical, the sound of glass shattering into a million pieces, not a muted thunk of splintered plastic.

But no matter. Either way I would have my woman.

Eve screamed as she scrambled for the door. I wish I could say I was too fast for her, but I wasn't. We both played our parts well. She was the petrified and bumbling victim; I was the ruthless pursuer. Yawn.

"Don't," she said when I grabbed her by the arm. "I'm pregnant."

I looked closely at Eve's stomach. She was five or six months along. Showing, but not huge.

Jackpot! And baby makes three. I'd have a brand-new family and a shot at happiness.

Then Eve said she was starving and hadn't had a bite in a while. So I bit her.

Just kidding. At least I have my sense of humor.

OH, BUT I did bite her. On the thigh. And her thigh was the fartiest of French cheeses, the briniest of anchovies. There was the thinnest layer of fat surrounding her muscle—clearly she had been a runner or tennis player—and it was enough to satisfy me. For the time being.

I chose the thigh for several reasons. First, it was firm yet still jiggly, the kind of thigh that looks good in short shorts. And I've always preferred the dark meat.

Second, a bite on the thigh would be out of sight. Even though my penis is as gangrenous as the rest of my extremities and sexual desire is but a dim memory, I still like to look at an attractive woman.

My final reason was Darwinian: I wanted to give Eve just a flesh wound, avoiding tendons and bones so she would have an advantage in our struggle for survival. When running from humans with guns or chasing humans with brains, every asset counts.

After the bite, I dragged Eve by her hair across the parking lot and toward a Mickey D's. Perfectly Neanderthal, I know, but desperate times. . .

We huddled in the restaurant's kitchen. It smelled greasy, repugnant. I never liked fast food as a human. That was for the obese proletariat. Let them have their Big Macs and heart attacks. I ate endive and goat cheese. All the same, there I was, scrunched under a fryer: hunted, haunted, and hungry.

And I still hadn't peed or shat.

Eve passed out immediately and when she awoke, I was writing. She put her hand over her unborn child and stared at me. She was growing paler. She would be with me soon.

Cue gothic screams. Cut to a shot of a deserted moor.

"What are you doing?" she asked.

I opened my mouth and out gurgled black blood and a low rumble.

"Can I see?" She held out her hand.

I clasped my notes to my chest like a teenage girl hiding her diary from her brother. I shook my head. Eve moved closer.

How I wanted her! I was a date rapist, Multiple Miggs smelling Clarice's cunt, Jack the Ripper, Josef Mengele dissecting his twins, the Zodiac Killer. The whole pantheon. I was out of control. Poe's Imp of the Perverse struck me and I was obsessed with one thought and one thought only:

Eat her, eat her, *EAT HER BRAINS*!

Dear God. Could a monster like me even have a mate?

Her hand was extended in a gesture of friendship. I noticed, for the first time, that she had a severe overbite, more than an overbite; her teeth were buck and coated with slimy plaque. I wondered what that plaque tasted like. When she opened her mouth, a string of saliva connected her bottom and top teeth. Little gobs of spittle collected in the corners of her lips when she spoke.

"Can I help you?" she asked. "You look, I don't know, scared or something."

Inarticulate brute that I am, I yowled in response. I sounded like Chewbacca.

"You can, like, write? Can all of you?"

She leaned closer to me and her hand, so transparent and thin I could see the blue veins underneath, touched the spiral binding of my notebook.

I moaned and bit that hand clean off.

Her bone stared up at me. Yellowish white but pure nonetheless. Blood gushed from her veins. I scuttled over to the cash registers and watched her as I ate her hand, which was ropy and bony. Far too scant for anything more than an appetizer.

Finger food is the punch line to this joke.

At least, I reasoned, if reason one can when crouched on the floor munching on a pinky, she would die and be resurrected sooner this way.

Her wrist was a geyser of blood, Old Faithful spilling onto the oily floor.

Soon the virus would staunch the blood flow, and by nightfall, the transformation would be complete. My bride and I could get on the road—two homeless zombies on a spiritual quest. Searching for our maker.

EVE WAS IN her final stages, incoherent, rolling on the floor, vomiting up her soul. The virus had devoured enough healthy cells to render her unfit for consumption. Utterly inedible.

My question: Why do I write? To be more precise, how am I able to write? I can't talk, I can hardly walk, and I certainly can't play the guitar. And yet I can hold a pencil, I can string letters and words and sentences together in a way that makes sense. This must be how the first caveman artist felt when his clan finally understood his hieroglyph meant water or hunter or sex or God. Are those not the basics? Man, woman, water, God.

And now add brains to the list.

If the virus melts the brain as they say it does, shutting down the frontal lobe, then part of my cognitive function is unaffected, uninfected. I either possess an innate resistance to some aspects of the virus or I am Zombie Adam, a bona fide mutation, the founding member of a new race.

In life, I wrote daily. I made my living writing articles, editorials, and books. I composed e-mails and PowerPoint presentations for my classes and colleagues. I occasionally blogged. Perhaps it's muscle memory. Is Stephen King still writing? Is Joyce Carol Oates? And the poets who squeeze out three lines a day—where is our Rimbaud?

History needed a zombie to record his experience. Call it creative nonliving fiction. We needed Ovid, Shakespeare, Herodotus. A poet to tell our side of the story. And since Johnny Cash wasn't coming back from the dead, it was up to me. Luckily, I was made for the job.

I felt expansive that night, filled with purpose. I forgave the humans for hunting me, as I forgave myself for eating them. Like Anne Frank, in spite of everything, I still believed we are all really good at heart.

AS I WATCHED Eve turn, I thought of Lucy. My human wife. The dam burst, and I remembered what happened to her. What I'd done. No wonder I repressed the memory; it was as painful to relive as an alien abduction.

Wretch that I am, I'd eaten her. All of her too. I can't believe I ate the whole thing. Every single morsel. She was good to the last drop.

Pass me a Tums, please; I've got indigestion.

We were sitting with the boxes of Christmas decorations—no

Hanukkah junk, mind you, no menorah, nothing Hebrew in sight—next to the never-used tent and Lucy's treadmill, also never used. We were in the basement with our life's detritus around us and my cheek was on the concrete and Lucy's hand was in my hair and I closed my eyes and I died.

Let that sink in: I died.

There was a moment of suspension when I was no longer human and not yet zombie. My body was nothing, was as good as a couch cushion or a blow-up doll or the giant plastic Santa mocking us in the corner. Walt Disney cryogenically frozen. Pinocchio before the breath of life, hanging limp from his strings.

It's true what they say about viewing your corpse from above. I floated near the ceiling, gazing at Lucy and what used to be me, and in that moment, I was as content as one of the Lord's sheep, a member of His flock. The zombie horde seemed far away; I could barely hear them pounding at the cellar door. My ears were flooded with celestial music, the singing of the spheres. It sounded like twee Britpop. Was it angels with harps? Maybe. Belle & Sebastian? Perhaps. Was it Jesus strumming an acoustic guitar like some traveling barefoot hippie? In my dreams.

Because let's rationalize: The whole "near-death experience," the whole light-at-the-end-of-the-tunnel trip, is a trick of the brain, a hallucination. It is not a supernatural event but one last fantasy brought to you by your endorphins to mitigate the absolute terror of death. To inspire hope against the nothingness we all fear. The whole cessation-of-ego-and-selfhood business. The loss of the world. Because everyone wants to exist, right? And we all die in the end.

Unless we're undead.

But then there are the suicides. Hanging themselves on reinforced beams in their empty Seattle apartments; overdosing on pills in their mothers' bedrooms; blowing their brains out with rifles or shotguns or pistols; starting cars in garages and reading Dostoyevsky until they fall asleep; driving minivans off cliffs with their children strapped in the backseat. They screw existence. In the ass.

Bear in mind, this is a zombie talking—a supernatural being. What do I know? I might not even be real.

Oh, ontology.

Regardless of religion or science, there I was, floating near the ceiling and at peace, when the heavenly music turned into Norwegian death metal and I was ripped away from the fuzzy blankets of cloudland and confronted with demons and devils and a descent into hell. I was whisked into some sort of meat tube, like a large intestine, where trapped souls screamed at me from polyp walls and everything was flaming orange and too hot. The guy from Munch's *The Scream* was there with his hands on the sides of his face. A child tattooed with the mark of the beast morphed into a stampede of wild horses running away from a gothic mansion that morphed into a laughing fat lady in pearls. The typical horror-movie shtick. Cliché, but true.

And then I was reborn.

Chew on that for a while.

Yea, though I walk through the valley of the shadow of death, I fear no evil. For I am evil. And I am the shadow. And I am death.

Not just zombie but archetype. Not just villain but hero. Jungian shadow, id and ego. Man is woman. Ovaries are testes. Cats are dogs.

Mr. Hyde was inside me clawing his way out. Dr. Jekyll was nowhere in sight.

I opened my eyes. And Lucy screamed. The zombie horde broke through the door and I lunged at my wife and my wife was lunch.

Heavens, she was tasty. We ate her communally: the fresh-faced blond zombette from next door; the nuclear family from across the street, which, as a result of decay, truly did have 2.5 kids; the haggard waitress zombie from Denny's, varicose veins now black and inky; the suspicious loner zombie who never gave out Halloween candy; the teenage geek zombie with his pimples and *Lord of the Rings* T-shirt; and me, the professor zombie, with my tortoiseshell glasses and robin's-egg-blue shirt.

This was no symbolic eating, no representational wafer. We didn't just break bread—we broke flesh; we drank blood. It was a living Eucharist.

Lucy's still in me now. Transubstantiation. Her remains remain. Forever and ever. Amen.

EVE AND ME, underneath the fryer. She was hot and feverish, barely breathing. Her skin was pale green, an anemic summer shoot. A fading spear of summer grass. That's Zombie Walt Whitman by the way. He never died either; look for him under your boot soles.

Soon the senseless masses would raid the rest stop. Whitman's catalogue of Americans: the farmer and the cobbler; the carpenter and the lunatic. The poet and the priest. Zombies, every single one.

I locked and barricaded the doors. Eve's moment of transformation was private; it belonged to us alone.

I FELT THEM before I heard them, before the humans even smelled their rot, their arrival heralded by a tingle in my shoulder, like when your foot falls asleep and you stamp it, waiting for the blood to return, the pinpricks to subside.

I welcomed the coming of the flock this time. I am more alive when I'm with them. We zombies are nothing more than a flesh-eating ant colony, but without a queen.

Because was anyone in charge? Could we even have a leader?

Death rattled like a snake in Eve's throat, and she closed her eyes. When she opened them again, I had my bride.

She was even whiter than before with a hint of sea-foam green. Her wrist had stopped bleeding; it was a scabbed and black stump, the bones poking through. They were thin and fragile looking, more balsa wood than dinosaur fossil. Girl could have used some calcium supplements. Of course, she didn't have to worry about osteoporosis anymore.

All she had to worry about was brains.

If my dick worked, we might have made love.

Urge and urge and urge—

Always the procreant urge of the world.

I fashioned a leash of sorts for Eve. In the frenzy of a feeding or while running from a lynch mob, I didn't want to lose her. The rope was tied securely around her chest, underneath her breasts and above the rise of her belly, and attached to my belt. I would've preferred to hold the rope in my hand, but I didn't trust my flesh. One good yank and my arm could fall off.

First things first: the wedding feast.

We left the McDonald's and headed for the Travel Center. Where chaos was king. Zombies were advancing toward the building in an unrelenting march; humans took potshots at their heads from the safety of the diner and gift shop.

Shambling, that's what the deplorable Max Brooks calls our gait. His book *The Zombie Survival Guide* was once shelved in the humor section of your local bookstore. Now every redneck and zombie hunter from here to California has a copy in his glove compartment and uses it as an actual survival guide. Every word turned out to be true. How's that for postmodern irony.

We exist in a season born of pulp fiction and video games, B movies and comic books. The word made flesh wound.

Any minute I expected to see Peter Cottontail hopping down the bunny trail with a basket of brightly colored eggs.

I led Eve back to the El Dorado—that mythic city of gold cum luxury Cadillac—and pacing around the vehicle was a man I took to be her husband. Or at least the father of the child.

Or, as I thought of him, wedding cake.

I pushed her out a few feet in front of me and hid as best I could behind her. Eve took a few steps forward, moaning.

"Susan!" Eve's lover cried when he saw her.

His eyes followed the rope connecting her to me. They took in her pallor, her shamble, her vacant eyes and inarticulate groans. He raised his rifle and aimed for her head. He grimaced and lowered the rifle.

I was betting baby would save us.

Lover was wearing a *Night of the Living Dead* T-shirt, which I took in the spirit it was no doubt intended—satirical, cynical, detached. Youthful, knowing, and hip, like being a 9/11 victim for Halloween 2001. Which I was. "Too soon," everyone at the party said, booing and hissing, when I showed up wearing a business suit and covered in dust. "Too soon."

"Oh, Susan," Lover cried again, his shoulders drooping.

Eve and I moved toward our first meal together. The eating of her former partner would sanctify our relationship, like the lighting of the unity candle. Nothing is taboo once you've scarfed down your lover.

He raised his rifle again and cocked it. He fired and hit Eve in the shoulder. She flinched but kept walking.

"Forgive me," he said as he recocked his weapon. "Lord forgive me."

I held my hands out in front of me like a statue of Jesus standing on top of the highest hill in some third-world village, His hands blessing the people below, protecting all. I opened my mouth to say, "Believe in me, my son, and you shall be forgiven."

"Moooooooorah," I said instead. Which was perhaps my most articulate moan yet.

He fired again and blew off Eve's ear. It flew past me, wavy and surreal, like van Gogh's ear. We're not zombies, I thought, we're artists. We're not artists, we're paintings. *Cannibalistic Sunflowers. Whistler's Zombie. Zombie Descending Stairs. Moaning Lisa.*

Eve and I fell on him. I wish I could say we were graceful as ballerinas, but ours is a clumsy, awkward race. Lover dropped his rifle. Eve bared her teeth in his face and he retched at her breath. It's a scene familiar to us all: Lovers in the morning turn to each other in bed, and both open their mouths to say, "Did you have any dreams, sweetheart?" And both pull back from the vestiges of last night's beer or cheesecake, the buildup of plaque, decay, and death in the other's mouth. A reminder that our bodies are science experiments, laboratories of bacteria. Ever-changing and evolving.

I let Eve take the first bite; she was, after all, eating for two.

Like a good little zompire, she went for the neck and hit the jugular. Blood spurted up, the money shot. She slurped the veins like lo mein, sitting back on her heels, her chin and mouth covered in blood, ropy sinews hanging out of her delicate overbite like this was the spaghetti-eating scene in *Lady and the Tramp*. A third of Lover's neck was gone. I grabbed his head and gave it a good turn and off it came. Lover's eyes blinked once, then his soul left the building.

I presented the head to Eve. She clutched its shaggy hair with her remaining hand and buried her face in the open end, bobbing for brains. I plunged my hands into Lover's stomach, ripped out the intestines, and shoved them in my mouth. They tasted like sour milk and I liked it.

I looked at Eve and she appeared to be smiling, but I couldn't be sure. Do dolphins actually smile? Dogs?

Fig leaf, I thought as I gazed at my bride. Serpent.

CHAPTER FIVE

WE REDUCED LOVER to his essence, a pile of bones and puddles of blood, then I struggled into the El Dorado. In spite of all I knew about zombies—the myths and realities, our limitations—it struck me that I might be able to drive to Chicago. If any cadaver could do it, I could.

The keys were lying on top of the dashboard, the gas tank was full, but I just sat there staring at the speedometer like a crash-test dummy. Behind the wheel, I was incompetent, as confused as an Alzheimer's patient puzzling over how to make a ham sandwich.

Disappointed, I got out of the car, and Eve and I shuffled to I-80 on foot. Soon enough we found ourselves in the middle of a herd of five hundred moaning, groaning corpses. A band of zombies is louder than you think. We gurgle, like giant rotting babies. An occasional limb hit the ground with a dull thud but everyone just shambled right over it. Zombies with broken backs dragged themselves across the blacktop, leaving trails of spinal fluid. The runts of the litter, those crips are lucky if they get to suck the bones of a kill.

I-80 was a junkyard. Vehicles with open doors and steaming engines. Bloody piles of clothes. The odd washing machine or Big Wheel. A stuffed Pink Panther. A desktop. A coffeepot. A dirty diaper. An algebra textbook and a Game Boy. The remains of

Western civilization. No cars passed us for an eternity. Eve walked in circles, bumping into other zombies. No one said excuse me.

As a human, I hadn't cultivated any sort of group affiliation or identification. In fact, I'd carefully avoided it. Being a lone wolf and an observer, an outsider with a melancholic disposition, suited my ideology and career. As an academic and cultural critic, I interpreted popular phenomena like NASCAR or reality television, but I certainly didn't consider myself a fan.

That's why my feelings surprised me: I felt a kinship with the creatures as we ambled down the road. I had sympathy for their hunger, compassion for their unquenchable thirst, sorrow when I looked at their maimed corpses. And I was worried about the future. Our collective ontology concerned me.

I practiced speaking as we walked, but I must have coughed up my vocal cords, if that's possible, and my tongue was a black and useless thing, a limp and charred sausage.

How could I discuss our survival with Stein if I couldn't even say goo-goo-ga-ga? For all I knew, Stein had become a zombie too. Just a slob like one of us. Crying for brains and covered with wounds that don't heal or weep.

"Eeeeeee," I said. Vowel sounds I could handle; consonants made me gnash my teeth.

The ground rumbled and shook. I pulled on the rope and brought Eve to me, inserting the tip of my finger into her wrist, which seemed to calm her. The unmistakable whir of a chopper filled the air.

Behind us, a military convoy crested the horizon. The American flag flew on the first tank, Old Glory waving in the wind.

This was why Eisenhower built these highways in the first place: to mobilize the military and evacuate citizens during an atomic attack. Black asphalt crisscrossing the contiguous forty-eight like bondage gear.

Never mind that most Americans took the highways to visit Disney World or dying grandmothers, not escape giant mushroom clouds and Russians. The roads brought us purple dinosaurs and snake farms. All-night diners and oil refineries. Buicks and monster trucks. The world's largest ball of twine. Cold War dreams turned millennial nightmare.

Better dead than red.

But better undead than dead.

Over fifty years after its construction, the System of Interstate and Defense Highways had finally fulfilled its original function. Mission accomplished.

Zombie Ike must be proud.

The tanks were accompanied by foot soldiers equipped with hand grenades, rocket launchers, submachine guns, pistols, flamethrowers, MREs, cigarettes, porn. And sharpshooters who went for the head.

Civilization hadn't completely broken down yet if the military was killing to the tune of "Walk This Way"—the Run-DMC version.

Doesn't anyone slaughter to "Ride of the Valkyries" anymore?

The soldiers opened fire. They were marching in unison, to the beat. They were, in fact, walking "this way," if "this way" meant the wholesale and rhythmic massacre of innocent American zombies.

I crooked my finger deeper inside Eve's wrist, hooked it around a bone, and pulled her closer. The other zombies were walking directly into the bullets. They simply couldn't comprehend the danger—they looked at the soldiers and saw only breakfast, dinner, a light snack.

My tribe is a stupid tribe, and that's precisely why I wanted to save them. To teach and lead them. But I couldn't do it if they wouldn't let me. It's like convincing your alcoholic girlfriend not to drink: It ain't gonna happen. Booze or brains, it's all the same. The addict has to want to change.

A nearby zombie's head exploded and a piece of his brains splattered on my glasses. His teeth flew out of his mouth and chattered down the highway. Eve took a hit to her swanlike neck, the chunk of flesh whizzing behind us so fast it whistled. My bride was falling to pieces under my care. I tugged hard on her rope and we took cover behind a Toyota Tercel.

THE CONVOY WAS easily a mile long, the middle guard a ragtag battalion of soldiers and civilians, Hondas and Beetles, motorcycles and skateboards. A young mother carried her baby in one arm and a machine gun in the other; a blond moppet of a boy skipped hand-in-hand with a cornrowed African-American girl, both throwing grenades into the zombie multitude. Humanity was finally united against a common enemy: us. Me.

This was genocide in front of my eyes and I couldn't stop it; my people were being extinguished like all the powerless masses of the world. Oppressed, dispossessed, hated. History teaches us that humans kill what they fear.

"Immigrant Song" came on at a lower volume than the Run-DMC, and the convoy stopped. In front of us was a giant cage on wheels, like the lion's cage at the circus, only bigger and pulled by a Hummer. There were zombies trapped inside, dozens of them at least, bumping into each other and clamoring at the bars. A small troop of battle-dressed soldiers walked alongside the corral, two of them on the side facing the Tercel.

I named them Rosencrantz and Guildenstern.

Here was the greatest tragedy of the twenty-first century. A viral outbreak and the military's bumbling response. Something was rotten in the state of Iowa. Or were we already in Illinois?

And was Britney Spears a zombie? Was the Dalai Lama?

The hammer of the gods.

Next to me, Eve thrashed around, foaming with desire. It was all I could do to keep her tethered; it was all I could do to keep from joining her in mad brain-lust.

Because just one bullet to the head and Jack Barnes would be dead.

"Don't even think about it," Rosencrantz (hereafter Ros) yelled as he rifle-butted a zombie poking his head through the bars.

"God, it stinks in there," Guildenstern (hereafter Guil) said.

"Fuckin' stenches," Ros said, and stumbled forward, moaning and pretending to bite Guil's shoulder.

"Cut it out, dude. You could get yourself killed."

"No one would take me for one of them," Ros said, and stood at attention, drawing himself up to his full six feet and squaring his shoulders.

"I meant by one of them, not us."

"Any soldier who can't successfully combat a zombie is a retard and deserves to be eaten."

Oh, how I wished I could bound forward like Bruce Willis, utter a snazzy one-liner, and devour the cocky bastard. Clearly that hubristic line signaled his demise. Anyone familiar with the grammar of film—not to mention Greek and Elizabethan tragedies—knows that.

Unfortunately Rosencrantz was right: I couldn't fight him with my restricted motor skills. And that depressed me. The military ranked lower than absurdists and *Everybody Loves Raymond* fans in my personal hierarchy of intelligence.

"Maybe," Guil warned, "but don't let your guard down. Always be alert and above all else, be prepared."

"What is this, the Boy Scouts? These corpses are slower than your grandma and mine put together. Bottom line: The war is over and the good guys won. Disaster, world takeover, zombie apocalypse averted."

Eve leapt, exhibiting a strength and agility far beyond what a pregnant zombie should possess. She dragged me around the Tercel and toward the soldiers. I tried to hold her back, hooking my foot on the bumper of the car, but the rope connecting us began to cut through my khakis and sink into my flesh. It could have slashed me in half—I was that decayed and soft—and then I'd be one of those pathetic crip zombies, dragging my torso around while my detached legs walked in aimless, undead circles.

Guil lifted his gun to his shoulder. "Die, zombie bitch!" he yelled, his finger on the trigger.

Ros hesitated. "Wait!" he said. "Check it out. That zombitch is preggie and she's dragging another one by a rope. What the fuck!"

"Whoa," said Guil, lowering his gun.

"We better take these guys prisoner. Call the corpse catchers."

Guil took a walkie-talkie out and spoke into it. "Two of them," he said. "Male and female. Not class-five aggressive, but not reduced to parts yet either. Moderate caution."

I struggled to hold Eve back. Her arms were outstretched, reaching for the soldiers, and she was pulling me with all her slight might. I fell to the ground, her ball and chain, dead weight.

"Uhhnnnnhh," she said.

Poor Eve, she'd really lost her looks since becoming a zombie. Her once-cute bangs were dirty and mottled with gore, and her eyes were filmed over, as haunting and evil as a vulture's. At times I wanted to gouge her eyes out; they reminded me of what I must look like.

I look like the rest of them.

As we rot, we become more alike. What was distinct and individual in life—a Marilyn Monroe mole, red hair, big breasts, Buddy Holly glasses, a penchant for making puns or wearing yellow suspenders—is erased and replaced with the shuffle, the moan, the torn clothes, the stink, the pallor, the dripping flesh, and the insatiable yearning. As we decay, we become one entity. United we stand. Or sway, rather.

"We have to hold them for a few," Guil said. "Catch crew is about a quarter-mile up the line."

"Looks like the male's doing that for us."

"You think that's his wife and baby? And maybe he's trying to keep the family together?"

I nodded my head at Guil's partial truth. In life, Eve had been a stranger. I wouldn't have opened the door for her at the mall. In death, she was mine, and I felt as responsible for the child as if I'd sired it myself.

"Holy shit!" Ros said. "Did that corpse just nod his head? Is he communicating with us?" He walked closer.

"Careful," Guil said.

"He's got her on a pretty short leash."

"It's not just her you gotta worry about."

Ros sidestepped the snapping Eve and approached where I lay on the shoulder, mashing my teeth into the white line, fighting for control. Because this was my opportunity to show the real me, the man beneath the animal. I watched Ros's combat boots approach. He knelt down.

He was young, not more than twenty, and he looked corn-fed, with freckles and a wide, flat face like a cow pie, only ruddy and pink. His hair was the color of dried corn stalks and his eyes were cornflower blue and bright.

Behind them was what I needed.

"What's up, fella?" he said, talking to me like I was a dog. "Can you hear me? Do you know what I'm saying? What are you doing with this here female and this rope?"

There was compassion in his voice. And the promise of help.

Stein, I tried to say, take me to Stein.

"Sheeeaiii!" is what came out.

"His eyes," Ros said.

"From here he looks pretty zombified," Guil said.

I rolled my head from side to side, shaking like an epileptic. I put my hand in my tweed jacket pocket and touched the papers there. My writing. Evidence of my cognition.

Ros was ten feet away. So close I could smell him. Everything in me sang: Brains for dinner. Brains for lunch. Brains for breakfast. Brains for brunch. . .

"I don't know," Ros said. "There might be someone home."

The zombies in the cage were watching; I could feel them cheering me on like binge-drinking fraternity brothers. We were tingling together, the ant phenomenon. My shoulder felt like a hard-on. A zombie orgy of sucking and smooching and licking and touching and brains and brains and brains and brains. . .

I withdrew my hand from my pocket, turning my back on salvation, and went for it. I wish I could say I attacked like a cat, even a fat old house cat, but we all know how zombies move. I crawled toward him, hand over hand on the pavement, baring my teeth.

"Looks like he's going for ya," Guil said.

Ros stood up. "Roger that. I'd hate to shoot this one, though. They'll want him for sure. Where are those fuckers?"

"I'm gonna slow him down," Guil said, "just in case."

"Roger that."

Guil tased me down the left side of my body, from shoulder to foot. My limbs twitched like a galvanized frog's. He turned the Taser on Eve.

"Watch the baby," Ros said. "They'll probably wanna check it out. I don't think we have too many pregnant ones, least not in this sector."

Guil nodded and zapped Eve's legs. She fell but continued pulling on the rope connecting us, single-minded in her pursuit.

Original sin. Eve did it again. She just can't resist temptation.

CHAPTER SIX

THE CORPSE CATCHERS came and the corpse catchers caught us. A rose is a rose is a rose.

A team of ten trotted toward us, looking like extreme butterfly catchers, wearing Kevlar, hazmat suits, and helmets, and carrying long poles, nets, and muzzles.

"Watch out for the female," Guil said to them. "She's more aggressive."

"Roger that."

I didn't resist or move. There wasn't much left at the site of my original bite. Strips of muscle clinging to the shoulder bone. I was only weeks away from being a dancing skeleton.

A catcher cut our rope.

"This is new," he said, looking at the frayed end.

"I'm guessing they did that in life," Ros said, "after they got bit, so they'd be together when they turned."

"Maybe, but he's more decomposed than she is."

I forced myself to my knees, then stood upright. I felt like Joseph Merrick, the Elephant Man. *I am not an animal. I am a human being. I . . . am . . . a . . . man.*

They covered Eve's head with their net and, using ten-foot poles, secured a muzzle over her. It looked medieval, like a knight's helmet but without the feathers and flourishes. They screwed the muzzle tightly around her neck with giant clamps. The woman in the iron mask, Eve clenched and unclenched her only hand. Her arms flailed as she groped blindly. I knew she was groping for flesh. Her corduroy maternity jumper—once as yellow as a lemon drop—was polka-dotted with dried blood.

The catchers led her to the cage; I had never loved her more.

"I am a conscious being," I longed to scream to the corpse catchers, to Rosencrantz and Guildenstern, to the world at large. "I love!"

"Uuhhhhnnnh," I moaned, and slouched toward them. Their net dropped over my head.

I stink, therefore I am.

CROUCHED IN THE corner of that stench-filled cattle cage, surrounded by rotters and moaners, our ontological state was clear to me: We were not men. Not any longer. But neither were we supernatural. Although we rose from the dead, we were not immortal. My pork shoulder attested to that.

Shortly after my capture, I made an attempt to distinguish myself. I crept up to the bars and held a note out to the guards, shaking the paper when they walked by. They ignored me, treating me like the others. And when I looked at my brethren, I realized why.

I was one of them, a member of the crowd, a zombie, nothing more, nothing less, helpless under the boot of this army.

EVE'S EYES CONTINUED to plague me. Pale blue with a hideous veil over them, they were the eyes of Terri Schiavo or Karen Ann Quinlan. Open but unseeing.

Why are America's most famous vegetables women? A year ago, I might have analyzed the female passivity and entrenched paternalism inherent in using women as national symbols for the chronic and persistent vegetative state. The "insertion" of the phallic feeding tube. The sexual connotations of the term "pulling the plug." The group of male doctors "stimulating" the patient to see if she "responds." I would have published the article too, maybe turned it into a book.

Now I only wonder: Does a vegetable's brain taste like broccoli? The soldiers had new lyrics for that old standby:

I don't know but I been told.
Fuckin' zombies ain't got no soul.

CORNFIELD AFTER PASTURE after cornfield after pasture after farm. Whenever a zombie appeared on the horizon, Ros and Guil took shots at him, her. It. If it was just one and they missed, they might let it go. If there were more, foot soldiers were dispatched while Ros and Guil stayed with us.

Illinois was devoid of the living. The convoy stopped often, sometimes remaining immobile for over a day. We heard gunshots, bombs, mortars, tow trucks moving cars off the highway. When we began moving again, fresh zombies were sometimes thrown in with us. Prisoners of war, they arrived frightened, hungry, and beaten by the military.

I overheard the guards say we were headed north to be studied and experimented on. Poked and prodded. We were special zombies, they snorted, a select few saved from extermination. The military deemed us worthy of further investigation.

But I didn't believe that claptrap any more than they did. My companions were stupid, lumpen zombies, as proletarian as chimney sweeps, some with guts hanging out of their asses and holes blown through their chests, all with that vacant stare. Eve was banging her stump against her head like an autistic brat and my fellow prisoners were reaching their hands through the bars, desperate for brains. The moaning had reached that peculiar pitch: the key of need. If the guards didn't feed us soon, there would be a riot.

After a few days, they brought us a meal. We all knew the meat was coming. My shoulder felt it first. Zombies began walking in tight anticipatory circles. Everyone was pulsing and electric, our bite sites connected as if by a live wire. Positioning myself near Eve, I fingered her stump and looked into her eyes. I wanted to communicate with her, to exchange a meaningful glance and delight together in what was to come, like newlyweds glancing at each other on their wedding night. But Eve's eyes were doll's eyes. Marble and flat.

I detested them. Eyes like stones.

I'm glad I ate Lucy. I'd hate to see her dulled, reduced to an object, a thing. A rabid automaton. Like a Meg Ryan movie, zombiehood would have offended her.

The guards threw the meat in the middle of the pack. It was a mixture of pig and cow, of guts, brains, bones, and hooves, and it was still warm with thick, wet blood. Like a wolf, I pounced on it.

So did everyone else. We fought over those brains Jack London–style: tooth and claw, club and fang. We fought like addicts over the final toot of coke. Piglets for teats. Holiday shoppers clawing each other for that last Tickle-Me Cabbage Patch Elmo Baby.

I had to win the brains to achieve alpha male status. I had to be king of the hill, at the top of the food chain. Because there is a hierarchy in zombiedom, however primitive: At the top is me, of course, standing alone, the smart zombie; next are the intact and the newly turned; slightly below them are those like Eve, older and a bit more decayed, but spunky and mobile still. Then come those with major injuries, gaping holes and broken legs or necks. The ladder continues downward in a predictable fashion until it hits rock bottom: disembodied legs and arms, crawling around like Thing from *The Addams Family*.

At least they have no eyes to haunt me.

I pushed the weak aside; I pulled hard on Mr. Businesszombie's arm and it ripped right out of the socket, ruining his pinstripe suit. Score one for Professor Zombie.

Surrounding the prime cut of brains was a football huddle of young strapping zombies. One still had a slight pinkish hue; he couldn't have been undead for more than a few hours. His hair hung over his eyes in a shaggy surfer wave, blond, silky, and straight. I nicknamed him Brad Pitt Zombie, and although he was muscular and handsome, I had something Brad Pitt Zombie lacked: cognition.

I wrested a leg bone from a feeble feeding group. Mostly children, they were lying down and suckling like grotesque kittens. Candy from babies. I held the bone aloft, arms raised to the roof of the cage, like the ape in the opening scene of *2001: A Space Odyssey*. I heard the movie's theme song swelling in the background as I swung the bone in a circle, sinking it into soft flesh, knocking down rivals. The triumphant drums pounded.

Thus Spake Zarathustra.

I battled my way into the middle of the huddle, gripping the bone like a baseball bat. A few zombies shuffled away; some continued feeding. I jabbed and poked and made caveman noises, scattering them all. Except for pink-cheeked Brad Pitt. He munched on those brains as if they were his due. Finally I took aim and smashed his pretty cheek, which split open, a perfect fissure like a fault line. He retreated.

I grabbed my prize, a brain the size of a basketball, and hobbled to a corner of the cage. Striking a defensive posture with my back to the wall, I sank my face into the spongy gray matter.

Aaaah . . . sweet mystery of life, at last I've found you.

When I looked up, chunks of brain clinging to my beard like canned ham, Eve stood in front of me. I ripped off a handful and extended it to her.

As she accepted my offering, a faint light flickered in her dead eyes. Call it respect. Call it gratitude. Call it victory. I called it love.

CHAPTER SEVEN

SUDDENLY AND LIKE that, the world was different. Reality shifted once again. Normal science was disrupted; weird science began.

Like they say in bad movies with cheesy voice-overs: That afternoon changed my life.

There was another like me.

The convoy had been stopped for a few hours; we were sated from the meat, although it wouldn't last long. Eating animal remains is like chewing Nicorette or shooting methadone. Ask any addict: Ain't nothing like the real thing.

I was reclining on the floor, absentmindedly sucking on a bovine spine. I was becoming quite a connoisseur of the fluid contained therein. It is bitter and salty, reminding me of oyster sauce and caviar. Eve was on her side next to me, her pregnant belly resting on the metal floor. Since I shared the victory brain with her, she had not left my side. She looked at me in a way I read as coquettish, but it was probably brutish and blank.

Oh, the lies lovers tell themselves.

Ros and Guil opened the gate. There was a minor scuffle as the corpse catchers struggled to contain the newbie. Ros and Guil shot at those trying to eat them, nailing a few in the head and dragging them out to be burned. I barely looked up from my bone.

"You corpses oughta like this one," Ros said as he turned the key in the lock.

I glanced her way and I was saved.

She stood in the center of the crowded cage, resplendent in a knee-length white dress, white stockings, white shoes, and a white cap perched jauntily on her gray bun. In her hand she carried a doctor's bag.

A simulacrum of a nurse; I didn't even know they wore those uniforms anymore. Of course, hers was torn at the shoulder and her stockings were stained with blood and a piece of finger clung to her bun, but that gave her the patina of a war nurse. Like Whitman.

She turned in a circle, assessing the scene, searching, I realized later, for the most critically wounded among us. And she found him: Brad Pitt Zombie. He was leaning against the wall, his cheek ripped open, revealing a bone to die for.

I felt guilty. My blow had been intended to "kill" a fellow zombie. But he simply wanted his evening meal just as I did. He was not my oppressor; humans were.

And didn't we all learn to share in kindergarten?

The nurse pulled a needle, thread, and swatches of fabric out of her bag. I walked over to her, Eve close behind me.

Her name tag said JOAN. A fitting name for a leader and a saint.

Joan stood next to Brad Pitt Zombie, so close that her Nurse Ratched breast touched his arm. Her bitten knee poked through her stocking; it was patched with suede. I bent down and touched it, rubbing the fabric; it was creamy and soft.

I dared to look up at her and my heart almost began beating again from sheer joy. Because her eyes were a miracle. Divine. The eyes of Pope John Paul II, Mother Teresa. Botticelli's Venus rising out of the ocean. There was light in them, a positive glow, a corona of higher cognitive function.

Brains! The woman had brains.

She cupped my chin and nodded. I grabbed her hand and kissed it, and she patted my head before turning her attention back to her patient.

Hallelujah! I would have wept, if zombies had tears.

I sat cross-legged on the floor and watched Joan work. She coaxed Brad into a sitting position by caressing his primary bite site, which was on his still-firm bicep. With her other hand, she pressed on his shoulder and he sat, docile as a baby lamb, while she worked her magic.

Her skill was immediately apparent, her fingers more adroit than most surgeons', let alone us uncoordinated zombies. She selected a black leather patch and sewed it onto Brad's cheek with an attention to aesthetics. Although the final result resembled some new S&M trend more than a post-op bandage, it would prolong Brad's living death.

Joan was a stout zombie with a curvy, matronly figure. A meaty hourglass shape. She was in her mid-fifties, I guessed, with what they call a handsome face—a square mannish chin, a prominent Mediterranean nose, and the puke-green skin of the not-so-recently turned.

It was love at first sight, and I worried the guards might recognize her as a threat, but they were intent on the horizon. What's more, the crush of corpses at the bars gave us privacy. The perimeter of our prison was at least two undead deep.

In my professor pocket, I had saved a brain treat. I wished I had a silver platter to put it on for her. She deserved better than my outstretched palm. Eve grabbed for the brains with her good hand and I slapped her away. Joan seized the golf-ball-sized chunk and swallowed it in one gulp.

"Mooooaaah," she said, licking her fingers. In zombish, that means thank you.

JOAN CARRIED RESURRECTION in her bag. Amongst the buttons and needles, leather and linen, there was rebirth and life, survival and hope. All three of the fates were in there too, weaving us into existence: Clotho spinning the threads, Lachesis measuring the length of our lives, and Atropos cutting the thread at the time of death.

Add a fourth fate to the classic trio: Saint Joan, old crone, spinster extraordinaire, sitting on her thanatopsis throne creating destiny for zombies.

My shoulder, once mere bone, was transformed.

When Joan rubbed her fingertips in circles on my scapula, it felt good and I understood how she rendered Brad passive. It was the most sensual experience I'd had since my transformation and I couldn't wait to touch Eve on her thigh.

After examining my wound, Joan put her finger to her lips and rested her chin on her thumb. I knew the pose well—it connotes critical thinking. Problem solving and decision making. Cogitation.

Together, we could help our people. We might even change the world.

Joan opened her magic bag and pulled out a hockey mask. A Jason Voorhees *Friday the 13th* mask. She shrugged her shoulders as if to say, what can you do? A slight smile crossed her lips.

O Captain! my captain! You have a sense of humor.

The mask was made of hard, sturdy plastic, the kind that is supposed to glow in the dark but rarely does. She wrapped the elastic straps underneath my armpit and sewed them into the flesh with string for good measure. My shoulder was secure and protected, and once I put my shirt and tweed jacket back on, it looked almost normal.

Jason on my shoulder was better than an angel. A monster on a monster, the hockey mask confirmed that our historical moment was unprecedented: Legend had become reality, fiction was finally fact.

Yes, Virginia, there really are zombies. Like Jason Voorhees, they rise from the dead.

JOAN COULDN'T TALK and neither could she read. I showed her my notes and she shook her head. Poor old gal. Illiterate zombie.

We devised a language, however, a signifying system of "natural" signs. Our communication was simple and childish: A pat on the tummy meant hunger. Nods and shrugs meant yes, no, I don't know, or whatever, depending on context. Making a gun with our hands meant Ros or Guil and making a cradle with our arms meant Eve or the baby. We scissored our fingers to indicate running or walking. And we tapped each other's shoulders to point out particularly idiotic zombies, the ones engaged in mindless repetitive actions like bashing their heads on the floor. A few of these unfortunates had eaten their own fingers, which resulted in horrible indigestion. They lay clutching their abdomens, vomiting up rivers of goo.

At least Joan could decipher diagrams, pictograms, and caricatures. These codes and signs held meaning for her. A drawing of a bull meant bull; a stick figure meant human; a slumped or lopsided figure meant zombie. I showed Joan a newspaper photo I'd found of Stein back at the Travel Center and she exhibited all the outward signs of comprehension. A thoughtful nod, a meaningful look, arms akimbo.

That was how I planned our escape. In pictures. I prayed I wouldn't run out of paper.

Saint Joan was like Jesus among the lepers; there were simply too many for her to heal. And some weren't worth it. With my help, she selected a choice group. Apostles, you could call them. We left the ones clutching the bars alone—we needed them to shield us from the guards, and anyway, they were thoughtless thugs, nothing more than meat-seeking missiles.

Our core group was small: Eve, Joan, Brad, and me.

And then came Guts.

Joan was examining Eve, pressing her hands and putting her ear on Eve's stomach. She must have heard or felt something, because she gave me the thumbs-up. Eve's primary bite site, her thigh, was in good shape as well. I tried to indicate to Joan that it was I who had bitten Eve and that I attempted to keep the wound small and contained in order to prolong her living death. I pantomimed the biting action, but the nuances were lost, and I don't know what Joan thought of our relationship.

Eve's wrist was a much more serious injury. To this day I regret losing control.

Joan was wrapping Eve's bones in gauze when Guts separated himself from the herd. His round brown face was spotted with scabs and pus like severe chicken pox, but his eyes were wide and white, not filmed over with the yellow mucus of the unseeing undead. He was only as tall as my waist; he would never get any taller.

He was stepping on his intestines.

Guts went straight to Eve's thigh and touched it. She leaned into his caress, closing her eyes. If she'd had breath, she would have sighed. But it was Guts's face that convinced me: This kid's a prodigy. He stays in the picture.

Cherubic doesn't go far enough to describe him. Neither does cute. He was every black street urchin in every TV show, from Buckwheat to Arnold. A child of the projects, wise beyond his years, spewing honest precocious wisdom to the foolish adults.

Of course, for all I knew he was more middle-class *Cosby* than ghetto *Good Times* in "real" life, but he can't contradict me. And I'm the one writing history.

Whatchu talkin' 'bout, Jack?

I'm talkin' superheroes, Arnold. This was my Team America, my own Justice League: me with my amazing ability to read, write, and plan; Saint Joan with her healing bag of magic; Guts with his empathic touch and alive eyes; Eve the maternal, the one who brings forth new life; and Brad, well, he was the expendable one. He would be the first to die again. He had only his life to offer the group and he'd make that sacrifice, if I'd read the script correctly. And I had.

Things were finally looking up.

Guts touched Eve's stomach and made a cradle out of his arms.

"Baaaay," he said. I nodded and tousled his braids, which were crusted with dried blood, leaves, twigs, and tiny lengths of veins.

I pinched Joan's elbow and pointed to Guts's guts. She rummaged in her bag, whipped out a roll of duct tape, pushed the guts back in, and motioned for me to hold them in place. They were dry and powdery, more like an old man's half-hard chalky dick than the wet, gooey, squishy, and delicious intestines of the living. Joan taped up his stomach, reinforcing the edges with her needle and thread. Good as new. No, better than new. Joan used embroidery thread, goldenrod, and it shone against his dark skin.

I spent the night touching Eve's thigh while she lay languorous and gloriously pregnant. Her stomach had grown and I planted my metaphorical flag on it, claiming it as England claimed India, as France claimed Africa. As America claimed the moon. I planned to teach all I knew to what was inside—not about linguistics or Walt Whitman or anything else academic, but about zombie slayers and triage healing. About surviving and leading. Issues of real importance, not hi-lo pomo masturbatory bullshit.

"Expecting" is an apt word for the state we were in. There was anticipation in the air. The baby filled me with a sense of potential and promise, a new beginning. I planned our future: Escape from this prison and find Stein. Under his protection, secure our right to exist. "Live" happily ever after. Roll credits.

Guts was curled next to Eve and me. Our hearts were stopped; we didn't breathe, bleed, sleep, or shit. We ate brains for breakfast, lunch, and dinner, but we were a family. Where there is love, there is hope.

CHAPTER EIGHT

THE CAGE REMAINED motionless for days. I didn't try to figure out why. I spent the time building alliances within the horde. Guts and I visited zombies with Joan and while she sewed up gashes and pushed eyeballs back in sockets, we fingered bite sites and fluttered our hands, flapping our arms like birds.

"Bird" as a symbol of freedom is a preverbal Jungian archetype; it's ingrained in human consciousness. Think Lynyrd Skynyrd's "Freebird"; the American eagle soaring high and "free as a bird"; think Maya Angelou's *I Know Why the Caged Bird Sings,* even Poe's oppressive raven; think the phoenix rising from the ashes.

Some of the more aware zombies appeared to understand that our gestures meant liberty and escape. A dim light shone in their eyes. Others were so far gone, it was useless. Probably dullards as humans as well, they were now catatonic brain-eating machines with no semblance of their former selves. Even fondling their bite sites produced only a mild reaction.

The guards were getting lazy. One day they simply herded a cow into our cage. A fat, lowing, and confused Bessie. With her long eyelashes, dewy brown eyes, and classic cow hide—white with brown splotches—she looked like an advertisement for milk.

"Don't have a cow," Ros said as he locked the gate behind him.

Oh, the way we fell on her. Bite sites on fire in a bovine gang bang. A revelry of blood and all those stomachs and did you know cow brains are very big? Which seems counterintuitive since there's not much thinking going on in there. The hide was tough and the skull was strong, but Joan whipped out her trusty scissors and plunged them into the heifer's head. All of us, fifty or sixty zombies, swarmed Bessie like ants on a corn dog, flies on shit, bears on honey, like any cliché you can think of.

"Look at 'em," Ros said. "It's hard to believe they were once human."

"There but for the grace of God . . . ," said Guil.

"Not to mention this assault rifle."

"God does help those who help themselves."

"Roger that."

Those fools. That aphorism's not in the Bible: *God helps those who help themselves*. Ben Franklin said it and it has since become the American creed, justification for American greed and unchecked capitalism. The Bible, on the contrary, the New Testament, more specifically, tells us to love our neighbors as ourselves and to feed the sick, the poor, and the hungry.

I stuck my hands into the hole Joan's scissors made, ripped open that cow's hide, and sank my face in. Like the frat boy I never was, I braced my hands on her horns and lifted my legs up over my head in a cowstand. My face was deep in her cranium, my forehead touching bone. I stuck my tongue out as far as it could go and licked.

It was bestial brainilingus and it tasted good.

When I put my feet on the ground, my tribe was watching—either in awe or stupefaction, it's hard to tell with the zombietariat. Eve walked over and licked the blood off my face. She and Brad were holding hands.

"Moohaaah," she said. I understood her to be expressing delight at my joie de mort and I tickled her wrist in return.

Turning my attention back to the cow, I motioned for Brad to grab hold of one side of the skull. I took the other and together we pulled at the bones. Others joined in—those who had been bandaged by Joan: a man in overalls, a woman in a summer dress, a butcher, a baker, a candlestick maker—and soon we were pulling as a team, a machine, a giant zombie nutcracker.

The skull came apart with a snap, revealing the jewel inside. A pearl, shining red, thick, and viscous. I grabbed the still-pulsing organ and held it over my head as if I'd just won an Olympic gold medal.

Brains, brains for all my friends!

AFTER EATING THE cow, we were one, and as one, we would escape.

The main obstacle was preventing my people from attacking the guards. If we advanced in our slow-moving way, arms outstretched for cerebrum, we would be shot handily. Our only hope was to surprise the guards, overpower them with our sheer numbers, and shamble away as fast as possible.

Zombies would die in the process. That's collateral damage. Ask any president or general. Study any war or revolution. Soldiers die. Innocents die. Winner takes all.

Operation Zombie Shield. I mapped it out, and like the best of plans, it was simple: The next time a newbie entered the cage, we would storm, en bloc, and shuffle out the door. Less-developed zombies concentrated in the front, in the back, and on the periphery; those with some cognition clumped in the middle, with the core group—Eve, Joan, Brad, Guts, and myself—snug in the center, protected, hopefully, by the mindless multitude surrounding us.

I showed the plans to the zombies who could focus on paper. They were crude drawings, stick-figure pictures even a child could understand. We also pantomimed the scene, with Guts playing the newbie and Joan a guard.

That Guts was a ham, a natural actor. His layers of reality were believable and complex—he "acted" more zombielike than he actually was: The light went out of his eyes, replaced by an exquisite expression of blankness. After the performance, his sparkle returned, just like that. The kid deserved an Oscar—or at least a Golden Globe.

Brad and I played peripheral zombies and I made sure to grab the walkie-talkie, represented by a cow bone, out of Joan's hand and throw it across the cage. It was essential to sever the military's line of communication, if only briefly. Every second would count.

I didn't know if the plan was communicated. The zombies were at least entertained by our performance, watching us like it was the Fourth of July and we were a fireworks display.

Oh! The best-laid schemes o' mice an' men (an' zombies).

Gang aft agley.

That's Zombie Robert Burns, by the way. His poetic apology to a field mouse he accidentally ran over with a plow. The poor rodent was chewed up and spit out. I hoped things would fare better for us.

JOAN, MY FIRST mate, Zombie Army's five-star general, our own personal Florence Night-in-hell, Joan had a bone to pick with Operation Zombie Shield. Joan had developed her own ideas.

As a matter of fact, Joan had a valid point.

Give these stench-wenches an inch . . . and they'll bite off your festering prick.

This was how we communicated: Joan pointed to my drawing of Ros bringing in a new prisoner and shook her head no. I shrugged my shoulders and raised my hands, palms up in the classic "Wha'?" gesture. Joan tapped her head with her finger, setting loose a large scabby piece of her temple, which she kicked aside with her nurse's shoe—no longer white, now rusted with blood.

With Guts playing Ros, Joan got down on all fours and lumbered around. She winced as her knee touched the cold steel floor of our moving cage and I felt a sympathetic twinge in my shoulder.

"Moooaaah," she moaned.

She was imitating a cow. Lord, she looked ugly doing it. Her conical breasts pointed straight down like stalactites. What had she been like in life? Was she married? With children? I imagined her as a brusque woman, bustling, efficient, and single. Suitors found her torpedo boobs intimidating. If not the breasts themselves then most certainly the bra, with its reinforcements, dominatrix straps and hooks, and impossibly large, pointy cups. Think Madonna circa 1992 but without the irony. You could poke an eye out with those things.

I made up a life for Joan: She was a woman whose career consumed her, filling the void of her loneliness. She lived near the hospital in an undecorated but immaculate one-room walk-up. She looked down on doctors, seeing them as bland faces with stethoscopes wielded like whips, and anyway, her diagnoses came quicker and more accurately than theirs, because she listened to patients. She expressed her disdain by dropping the definite article when referring to doctors, as in "Doctor will examine you shortly."

As in, zombie will eat your brains shortly. Would you like a magazine while you wait?

It was obvious Saint Joan wanted us to attack and make our escape when the guards ushered in our next meal, not the next prisoner of war.

I shook my head no.

She tapped her wristwatch and spread her arms wide like she was telling a fish tale. And I'll say it again: She had a point.

The cage was full—at overcapacity, federal-prison levels of occupancy—and the guards hadn't brought in a newbie for days. In fact, we'd been moving for a solid day, which was unusual. I nodded at her and tapped my head, indicating I'd think about it. She wagged her finger at me, then pointed to Eve's belly—which was ready to pop. Eve was looking corpsier than ever and her stomach was moving, the zombino within writhing like an alien about to explode.

Eve could not have the baby in captivity. No child of mine would be born a slave.

Saint Joan was right. We had to escape immediately. Whichever came first: cow or zombie. I had to set us free.

Move over, Moses. Step aside, Joseph Smith. There was a new prophet in town.

Pharaoh, let my people go!

CHAPTER NINE

JUST A FEW short hours after my conversation with Joan, there was a commotion. Ros and Guil were whooping and laughing; superior officers came rushing down from the front of the line. A high-ranking general arrived by helicopter. I inched toward the bars, Guts following close behind. The dead stepped aside for us; such was my influence.

America's favorite daytime television talk-show host stood outside our cage, trapped in the corpse catcher. Although her neck was in the steel encasement and her arms and legs were shackled, her head was left uncovered. She had the complexion of the undead and her lips were cracked and coated with dried blood, but her hair was coiffed to perfection, not a strand out of place.

We must be near Chicago, I thought. Stein's home base.

Lucy had been a fan of her show and I'd seen it once or twice, rolling my eyes as she nattered on about chemical peels or health care reform, Tom Cruise or her favorite scented soap. Both the president of the United States and the winner of the Westminster dog show had been on her couch, and as far as I could tell, she treated them with equal importance. Lucy thought she was a woman of the people, a hero. A self-made Queen of All Media.

The Queen was currently biting at the air, snarling and foaming; through it all, she still looked regal.

"Watch out, sir," Ros said to the general, "she's a fighter."

"You think I can't handle a zombie, soldier?" the general asked Ros.

"No, sir." Ros gulped.

The general thrust back his shoulders. He had a crew cut and his uniform was pressed and clean—too clean for the dirty business of rounding up zombies. His medals shone in the sun.

"What did you say?" he asked.

Here was our chance: Take one smug officer who lives at his desk, put him to the test in the field, and watch him fuck up.

"I said no but I meant yes, sir. At least I think I meant yes."

"He meant you can," Guil put in, "handle a zombie."

"Right," Ros said. "Absolutely, you can absolutely handle a zombie, sir. Just please, sir, don't get too close. You have to be careful of their spit. It's toxic. Sir."

"Son, I've been handling zombies since before you were born."

"With all due respect," Guil said, "that's impossible, sir." He took off his helmet. His black hair was knotted against his head, as if it hadn't been washed in weeks.

The general waved his hand at our cage. "If not zombies per se, then gooks, A-rabs. Same difference. Enemies. Insurgents."

"Yes, sir. Just be careful. Zombies are a new breed."

Our brains, I realized as I watched Guil comb his fingers through his hair and replace his helmet. We needed to protect our brains. It was the only way to escape unscathed. I nudged Guts and pointed to the helmet, then mimed putting it on my head. He nodded.

"Not so important now, are you?" an infantryman said, and threw a rock at the Queen. It hit her in the head and she turned toward the soldier, barking like a dog. The corpse catchers held tight to their poles, one at each limb like she was being drawn and quartered.

"Get back to your station," Ros said, "before I kick your ass back. We'll have none of that here."

"I hate zombie bitches," the young man muttered as he walked away, "especially black zombie bitches. Excuse me, African-American zombie bitches."

I rubbed Guts's shoulder in sympathy. Racism and sexism are ugly enough without adding zombism to the mix.

Oh, hateful, hateful humans.

"Sorry for that, sir," Ros said to the general. "The men have been under a lot of pressure lately. Everyone has."

"It's to be expected," the general said, "during wartime. They're only human." The general pointed to the Queen. "And she's not."

"Woo-hoo!" one of the corpse catchers said. "But what a catch! Are they gonna give us a commendation or what? Maybe get interviewed on TV."

"I watched her show every day with my mom," another said, shaking his head. "And to see her like this, it just breaks my heart."

"Where'd you find her?" the general asked.

"Over by the train station."

"We didn't know who it was at first. She had her face stuck in a dog. All we could see was her dress and that hair."

"Stuckey was gonna go ahead and shoot, but I thought the hair looked familiar."

"I fired in the air," Stuckey said. "She looked up and I got a good look at her face. Even with the dog fetus hanging outta her mouth, I recognized her. Ha! Crazy goddamn world."

"Mooaaahhhh!" said the Queen.

"Better corral her," Guil said.

"Negative," the general said. "I've ordered a photographer, should be touching down any minute, and I intend to corral this particular zombie myself. Take some souvenir pictures. For the wife, the papers, posterity, that sort of thing."

"Like Abu Ghraib?" Ros asked.

"You're in dangerous territory, soldier."

I found myself liking Ros more and more. Cheeky bastard.

GUTS AND I rushed back to Joan, Eve, and Brad. We had to mobilize the crew before the photographer arrived. We had to execute my plan.

I stood in the center of the cage, Guts on my shoulders, the hockey mask protecting my injury from his little leg. And Guts, the star, the natural born leader, he laid out the plan, gesturing with his hands for the dumb zombies one last time.

To hold their interest, I threw out bits of brain I'd stored in my professor pockets. Saint Joan did her part, walking among them, caressing bite sites, securing bandages, sealing up holes. She was a born healer. I spied Brad and Eve mingling with the masses, holding hands. Young undead in love; I'd lost her to him.

No matter. I had a people to save. Freedom to secure.

We heard the whir of a helicopter and I made my way back to the bars. The photographer ducked under the chopper's blades; she was in her twenties, with short bushy hair and wire-framed glasses. Touched with the beauty of youth, she was chunky in all the right places, like a thick cut of chuck roast—the strips of fat are the tastiest part.

The general held out his hand for the corpse catcher's pole while the photographer read her light meter and lined up angles. She had both a thirty-five-millimeter and a digital camera and she started snapping away, her thighs pressing against her khakis like trussed-up turkeys.

She turned her lens on the cage. Instinctively I smiled. She brought the camera down to her waist and we made eye contact. I winked.

"General," she said, "I think that zombie just smiled and winked at me."

"Nonsense," Ros said.

"A trick of the light," said Guil.

"It's what you want to see," Ros said.

"A projection," Guil said. "Like anthropomorphism."

I backed away from the bars and took my place in the center of the group. Guts scurried around our legs, positioning zombie elbows, fingers, and hands on bite sites. We had to be connected. We had to throb as one.

Saint Joan was next to me. My knee touched her knee and her hand was on my shoulder. We tingled, an army of red ants itching for a fight.

The door opened to let in the newbie and we moved forward in tight formation.

"Is this normal?" the general asked.

The camera clicked in rapid succession.

"What the fuck?" Guil said.

"Who bandaged them?" the general asked. "Is that SOP?"

We advanced. Guil fired at us.

I heard the squawk of a walkie-talkie and Guts ran forward like a sprite, revealing his true superpower: He moved with the speed and agility of a human. When he returned, he handed me the device and I turned it off. How he wrested it from the guard, I'll never know.

We moved forward, slow and sure. Methodical monsters. Zombies fell in front of me, shot in the head. We stepped on them. They made a soft carpet.

"I can't control her!" the general said. "I'm losing her!"

The general dropped the long pole with a clank. The Queen of All Media picked it up, wielding it like nunchakus. She swung, missing the general but ramming the remaining three corpse catchers. The men fell down.

"Shoot her!" someone yelled.

"Negative! Hold your fire!" the general said. "That's our prized catch. She is to be taken alive. That's an order!"

"Actually," Ros said, "I believe undead is the word you're looking for."

"I've had enough out of you!" the general yelled.

The Queen was free. With a pole in each hand, she knocked down Ros and Guil. Their guns clattered to the ground. Guts sprinted up, kicked the walkie-talkies and guns out of reach, and removed Ros's helmet. The general fired and hit Guts in the back, but the urchin barely flinched. The general fired again and hit Ros in the arm. The soldier rolled in pain. Guts ran back to my side and presented me with the helmet, which I immediately donned. It had a Blink-182 sticker on it.

Brad Pitt Zombie, inspired, perhaps, by the bravery of Guts, stumbled forward and removed Guil's helmet. Someone shot Brad in the head and his brains exploded in a star-spangled display of gore. Guil ran for cover.

"Noooooooooah!" Eve moaned. It was the closest to language I'd heard from her, such was her grief.

Emboldened by the protection of my brains, I grabbed Guil's helmet out of Brad's stiff arms and gave it to Joan, my second in command. Ros was lying on the ground a few feet away, shot and helpless, and, Lord forgive me, the timing was all wrong, my attention should have been on the melee and the escape, but the urge, the urge, the urge, always the procreant urge . . . I bit him on top of the head, scalping him.

Ah, creamy nougat of live human flesh, I adore thee. A thousand times better than cow or rabbit. Ros screamed. Guil ran to his side.

"Shoot me," Ros said, clutching his friend's collar.

"How could I?"

"Death is not anything. Death is not . . . ," Ros said.

"Life?"

"Death is the absence of presence. But living death is . . ."

"The presence of absence?" Guil said.

"But do I want to die?"

"Why would you?"

"Perhaps life as a zombie is better than no life at all," Ros said.

"Roger that."

The photographer ran away, her sweet fat untasted. The general fired aimlessly, pointlessly, until he ran out of bullets, stopped to reload, and was attacked by the hive. The general had read the script. He knew his part: corpulent, arrogant, dinner.

I took a few moments to chew on Ros's hairy head while listening to him and Guil prattle. Gunshots whizzed around me. Humans emitted their death shrieks. In the distance reinforcements were running toward us, firing away.

"Wait with me, old friend," Ros said. "The future."

"The future?"

"It's murky."

"It always is."

The Queen snuck up behind the babbling pair and bit Guil in the neck, making it official: Rosencrantz and Guildenstern were undead.

Oh, gotta love those allusions.

Stringy veins hung from the Queen's mouth like bean sprouts. I looked into her eyes; no one was home.

I left the three of them and pushed my way through the feeding frenzy surrounding the general. Zombies fell away, bowing as I marched past, paying homage to their liberator.

I was commanding as much respect as Jesus Christ on Palm Sunday. Wrap your juicy brains around that.

The general's head was cracked open, brains exposed, helmet on the ground next to him. I grabbed a fistful of the gray matter and stuck it in my pockets. I also extracted his liver and a layer of blubber from his stomach—who knew when we'd feed again?

I gathered my family and bestowed the general's helmet on Eve, securing the straps underneath her weak chin. Only Guts was left unprotected.

The reinforcements were almost upon us. The Queen stepped between us and them, waving her arms like Vishnu, the poles still attached. Destroyer. Preserver. She stopped them in their tracks.

"Holy shit, bro, is that who I think it is?"

She swung those steel octopus arms and knocked a few soldiers down.

They shot her in the head, and she fell to the ground.

Even the great tumble.

As for us, we ran, shambled, hobbled away. A bullet pinged off my helmet but did no damage. We looked at the road ahead of us. We didn't dare turn around and look back.

CHAPTER TEN

AT A REST stop near DeKalb, we spotted two young humans looting a Kum and Go. I felt sorry for the critters; they couldn't have been more than ten and they were completely vulnerable. The easiest of prey, they might as well have been wrapped in plastic in the meat department of your local grocery store. No weapons, no strength, no adult protection; it's a wonder they were still alive. The girl clutched a package of Zingers; the boy held a Twinkie.

No bell dinged as we entered the store; the electricity was out. Joan locked the door behind us. The kids tried to run, but we circled them like cavemen; on my signal, we attacked.

I watched Guts closely but discerned no negative effects from eating someone his own size, a child he might identify with. Joan and Eve displayed a lack of sympathy as well. Each bit, slurped, and bit again with relish.

There was no reason to feel guilty, I rationalized. Jesus served his own flesh and called it communion. What is the transubstantiation if not cannibalism? The raising of Lazarus and Jesus's own resurrection: ancient zombie activity.

And the guy who started it all, YHWH, god of the Old Testament, He lived to smite the enemies of Israel, demanded the sacrifice of lambs and rams, and turned Lot's wife into a pillar of salt just for fun. Righteous, vengeful, and jealous as all hell, He asked fathers to murder their sons and ate firstborns for dinner. Just as we did.

I caught a glimpse of our gang in the round security mirror as we sat on the bloody floor, hunched over body parts. A swatch of stone-washed denim clung to the human girl's thigh. A rack with Bubble Yum, Cheetos, and other brightly packaged junk food loomed over us. Eve's stomach was huge.

Clearly, the Lord was on our side; we were made in His image.

I made sure there were leftovers, putting a few toes, ligaments, a stomach lining, and an ear in Ziploc bags before hitting the road.

Isaac, I decided, patting Eve's belly and feeling all biblical. Boy or girl, the baby would be called Isaac.

AFTER WALKING NORTH for days, we came upon a sculpture garden of chain-saw art created by a human-turned-zombie named George Kapotas. Chicago was less than a hundred miles to the east.

Kapotas had been a religious man, and the bulk of his own private Eden depicted the life of Jesus: the virgin birth in the manger attended by wise men and camels; Jesus, suddenly an adult, preaching the word and petting a lamb; the Last Supper as imagined by da Vinci; and the pièce de résistance, the crucifixion, with all three crosses and the wound in His side.

Jesus Christ Superzombie, the whole Passion Play, chainsawed out of trees.

In addition to his devotional work, Kapotas carved bears, raccoons, and American Indians with his chain saw. Woodland creatures were scattered among the religious tableaux, making for a peculiar vision of the Holy Land. There's Jesus healing the lepers and behind him, climbing a tree, is a koala bear. And Jesus chilling with John the Baptist, both of them leaning against totem poles.

When we stumbled in, George Kapotas's chain saw lay impotent at his side, and his head was inside the torso of a small child, sucking the last specks of meat from its rib cage.

I pulled an ear out of my professor pocket and bit into the cartilage, studying the grunting, moaning folk artist. We would hide out in the Garden of Eden until Isaac was born. I signaled as much to my comrades and they made themselves at home.

BESIDES BEING A chain-saw sculptor and religious nut, Kapotas had been a ham radio operator. Guts and I found a modest setup in the garage while exploring and securing our fortress.

First signal I picked up, we heard this: "Moooaaaan. Ohhhh-nhnn." Silence. Then, "Mooohhanaa."

Radio Free Zombie.

Guts turned the dial and picked up some joker out in Lawrence, Kansas, calling himself DJ Smoke-a-J and spinning Roky Erikson's "I Walked with a Zombie" as well as songs by Rob Zombie—solo and with White Zombie—the Cramps, the Misfits, Ghostface Killah, and My Chemical Romance. Even that old standby "The Monster Mash."

In life, I would've written an article about the fool and his broadcast. Postapocalyptic stoned DJ waxes postmodern with songs that spit cynically in the face of his life-or-death situation. The title would be: "The Living Death of Irony: How Pop Culture Illuminates and Comments on the Current Zombie Crisis."

If only DJ Smoke-a-J weren't so goddamn pathetic. He introduced the oldies classic "She's Not There" by the Zombies with this: "I feel bad and I'll never forgive myself, never fuckin' ever, not in a million years, but I hid in the closet and listened to zombies eat my baby girl. She was only two years old. Meagan. And . . . and . . . God, I can hardly believe I'm saying this, but one of the zombies doing the eating was her mother. I tell myself I had no choice in the matter. It was the baby or me. And I chose me. Sweet Jesus, I chose me."

DJ Smoke sobbed for a bit and Guts grinned in a way that was evil, if an adorable zombie urchin can be evil. Finally Smoke took a big breath and continued, "So . . . I guess Meagan's not there either. And neither is her mother. I mean, they are in that they exist, sorta, but they're not really there. Like their minds aren't there. Just like the girl in the song."

Cue music. It was enough to make a flesh-eating zombie weep.

Guts started to break-dance and wiggle when the chorus rang out: *Let me tell you 'bout the way she looks. The way she acts and the color of her hair.* He was bouncing around the garage, kicking his legs high in the air, throwing his hands up like he just didn't care. He snapped his fingers—and a chunk of his thumb flew off. I picked it up and handed it to him, signaling that he should go visit Saint Joan by making pointy breasts with my hands and simulating sewing the top part of the thumb back on. He gave me the thumbs-up—his poor digit only half there, the tissue moldy green and coagulated with black blood—and skipped out.

I was glad to give Joan something to do. And glad to be alone.

Finding Stein suddenly seemed impossible, a needle in a haystack, a wild goose chase. I needed information, Stein's exact location; I needed Google and MapQuest. I needed a reliable search engine and the glut of the Internet.

I wanted my MTV. I wanted CNN and *Larry King Live*. And there was only the radio; Kapotas didn't even have dial-up—no desktop in sight. When I turned on his television, there was nothing. Not a test pattern or the bleat of the Emergency Broadcast System.

I still didn't know who was winning the war, but with mass communication down, I suspected it was a draw. And as anarchic as World War III.

There had to be other zombies like us, small groups of them scattered across the country, challenging the hegemony of the humans. Drawing their own escape plans and fighting for their existence with intelligence and forethought.

The big question was: Where were they?

I turned the dial: "The rapture is here, brothers and sisters! Hallelujah! Those who have sinned against God—the homosexuals, the abortionists, the atheists and rapists—they are the living dead. They walk among you, eating your children. God is punishing us for our wickedness. These creatures are demons and sinners, and they want to drag you down to the fires of hell with them. They want you to decay and rot and cannibalize your own family. But Jesus will protect you, hallelujah. Those who accept Him into their heart, those who truly believe in Him, will be spared. Yea, though I walk through the valley of the shadow of death, I fear no evil for the Lord is with me."

I turned the dial again. Static.

WE STARTED AN exercise routine at the Garden of Eden. Mind, body, and spirit.

Because when I returned from the garage, I found Eve and Kapotas doing the zombie dance around the crucifixion scene. Walking in no particular direction, drooling, moaning, eyes and minds empty as seashells, heads banging against the chain saw–carved crosses.

Tabula rasa. Tabbouleh for brains.

I signaled to them, waving my arms and jumping up and down, but it was as if I didn't exist. I was not only zombie but ghost as well. The Invisible Man.

"Eeeeoooaaah," I said, which meant: "Hellooo. Anyone home? Earth to zombies!"

No reaction. Kapotas rubbed his head against the robber's cross, while Eve fell to the ground, her hands holding her stomach, which had grown so large and roiling it looked like her skin might rip apart.

Kapotas was a hairy zombie. He was covered with the stuff: black, oily, on his arms, legs, back, and belly, like a bloody teddy bear. And he was stocky, with stubby arms and legs and a barrel chest. He looked like the type of guy who's comfortable using a chain saw—for creation or destruction. Kapotas's primary bite site was on his neck, which was so thick it was barely there. Joan had sewn the wound up with sky-blue embroidery thread; it looked like a spider's web. I stuck my finger in its center, grabbed Eve by her stumpy wrist, and led them to the courtyard, where Joan and Guts were looking up at the clouds.

The problem with zombies is they're incapable of entertaining themselves. Leave them alone for a few hours and they become despondent and depressed, staring at the wall, dreaming of brains and guts and brains and guts and brains and brains and. . .

I lined them all up in a row and led them in a series of calisthenics. Hands over heads, reach for the sky! Hands on the ground, touch your toes! Nothing too strenuous; I didn't want any body parts to fall off. They all did as I asked them to, even though Joan was so stiff with the rigor she could barely bend at the waist and Kapotas and Eve needed to be bribed with brain-treats to keep from wandering off. Those two weren't any smarter than dogs, but, like dogs, they could be trained.

Besides, the best soldiers are the dumb obedient ones. And that's what I wanted. An army. A Zombie Army to limp our way to victory.

It was a long shot, but long shots don't stop heroes. Think Sitting Bull standing up to Custer; the Allies invading the beaches of Normandy; think Luke Skywalker destroying the Death Star and David slaying Goliath.

This was my plan: gather a militia and storm Chicago. We had the element of surprise on our side. That's why we succeeded with Ros and Guil; they never expected an organized attack from corpses. Once inside their perimeter, we'd grab hostages and take over a tank, using force, the only language the military understands. After we had their attention, we'd request an audience with Doctor Stein. Violence would give way to diplomacy when Stein perused my document, an elegantly worded and passionate plea to his sense of equality and justice. With my background and knowledge, I would write an argument as persuasive and historic as "Letter from a Birmingham Jail" or the Declaration of the Rights of Man.

First the power of the sword, then the pen. I'd be hailed as a savior. A leader. Thomas Jefferson. A king.

I put the chain saw in Kapotas's hands, hoping to jar his memory. A weapon like that could be an asset in the revolution, especially wielded by a resolute cadaver. I pulled the ripcord and it sprang to life, roaring *Texas Chain Saw Massacre*–style.

Kapotas dropped it and sliced off his own foot at the ankle.

"Noooaaaahmmmm!" he said, reaching out to his appendage, which hopped away on its own volition, going who knows where.

Zombie Army's first foot soldier.

Doomed. I put my head in my hands. We were doomed.

I WAS WITH Eve in the Garden of Eden, my hand on her thigh. The serpent hovered above our heads. Chain-Saw Eve clutched the apple in her hand, already won over to the dark side. My Eve nibbled on an olive-green toe.

Her eyes were getting worse. Filmy and yellow, like faded gauze curtains, they were as dead as Kapotas's Eve—and she was carved from wood. We were down to the last of our provisions: digits, skin, fat, blood. Everyone was desperate for viscera. If I didn't secure brains soon, my army would go AWOL looking for some.

Earlier that day, the president had been on the radio. I was shocked that we still had a president. And it was still the same guy.

"My fellow Americans," he said, "we are in a crisis of biblical proportions. Basic services are down and many citizens don't have electricity or running water. There are no police forces or hospitals to, uhhhh, provide protection and administer aid. As a matter of fact, we're unsure how many of you are receiving this broadcast. Or how many are left alive.

"Although I have declared martial law to restore order, for the most part you are on your own. We are in the process of rebuilding infrastructures and getting food and water to those who need it. But the problem is finding you without attracting attention from the enemy. And that's a hard job. We work very hard at it.

"The enemy is crawling all over our great nation, from Portland, Maine, to Portland, Oregon. Our intelligence suggests it's Armageddon, as foretold by the Book of Revelation. In other words, Judgment Day.

"We are sure, positive, there is no doubt, that one of the prophecies has come true: The dead walk among us. And they're zombies.

"These are extraordinary times requiring extraordinary measures. I understand vigilante groups have been formed. I support this. I also support citizens, uhhhh, *gathering* supplies from stores and supermarkets, as long as it's done in an orderly fashion. I urge

you to bond together and help your neighbor. Reach out to one another. And above all else, pray together.

"Not since 9/11 have the American people stood stronger or
firmer. I am proud of your conduct and courage. God bless you all.

"Our military commanders have given me some practical advice
to pass on to you: Never forget the enemy. If you see one, don't approach it or talk to it. Even if it's your father. Because it's not your
father. Not anymore. Shoot it in the head or burn it. It's essential to
destroy its brain.

"Let me repeat: If you don't have a weapon, do not approach the
enemy. Walk away as fast as you can. You may even want to run.
Find a structure, make sure it's not infested with the evil ones, then
secure it and protect yourself. You have the full support of your president to do whatever it takes to survive. Any means necessary.

"Rest assured that your government is working toward a swift
resolution to this crisis. The full power of our military has been de-
ployed. Congress has declared war and given me the authority to use
extreme force—and that includes nuclear force.

"Stay safe, stay together, and stay alive. God bless America."

"The Star-Spangled Banner" came on. The president had men-
tioned nuclear war, another kind of apocalypse.

Contacting Stein became more important than ever. With compel-
ling rhetoric and a receptive audience, I could speak for my people,
represent our point of view. Maybe even end the war.

First things first: I had an army to feed.

CHAPTER ELEVEN

MY FATHER NEVER took me hunting. Dad and I read and discussed books together. We visited museums and cafés. He taught me how to swirl brandy and smoke a pipe. All the splendors of old Europe.

"The forest is a primeval place," he said, "where ticks suck your blood, brambles scratch your legs, and rednecks lie in wait for people like you and me."

"Like you and me?" I asked.

"Jews," he said. "Intellectuals. And the blacks too. The rednecks are not fond of them either."

As a child, I thought rednecks were creatures with bright red necks, like the tropical birds I saw at the Central Park Zoo. It was years before I realized they were just people, not monsters with bulbous necks hiding behind trees in woods.

Now I'm the monster, lying in wait for a fat red neck. Tables turned.

Guts and I trudged along the highway on our hunt. I put my hand on his helmet. He looked up at me and when I gazed at his undead visage, a surge of emotion swelled in my chest: his sunken and watery eyes, the blackened strip of his tongue, the chicken pox scabs pulsing greenly. I felt paternal and tender toward the tyke, maudlin even, and I understood the love my father held for me: unconditional and pure, selfless, and without a trace of irony.

It made me wish Lucy and I had created a child.

There was a rustling in the overgrown wildflowers in the median. We heard moans and chattering, giggles and nonsense. Two heads emerged from the tall grass.

Zombies Ros and Guil.

"Brains," Ros said.

That voice! Musical, yes, and a miracle too, for it was a zombie talking. Talking! It was deep and guttural, Barry White singing in a tar pit, the devil speaking through Linda Blair in *The Exorcist*.

"Br . . . buh, buh, bray. Mmmmmm," said Guil, and he sounded as primal as the rest of us.

The soldiers looked worse for the wear, but whose looks improve after death? Ros's cranium was exposed, but besides that he was in one piece. Guil was in much worse shape; his head fell to the right, resting on his shoulder like a broken jack-in-the-box. The neck veins and muscles hung out like stuffing.

Clearly, they needed Joan—and Zombie Army needed them.

Ros pointed at me.

"You!" he wheezed.

Gadzooks! Not only did he talk but he had a memory to boot. Triple hallelujah!

"Bwaaaaahmmmmnoh!" I shouted, and rushed to Ros. Arm extended, I stuck my finger in the top of his head, tickling the edges of the bite.

His eyes rolled back. He looked like Ray Liotta in *Hannibal,* the scene where Anthony Hopkins eats Liotta's brains while Liotta is still alive. It's both a lobotomy and a feast.

"Gooood," Ros said. "Hmmmmm."

With my other hand I touched Guil's neck, where he'd been bit less than a month ago. The three of us stood there for a few minutes, locked in the zombie embrace, a mangled ménage a trois. Guts skipped around our legs like an oversized puppy.

A crow cawed high above us. Ros put his hand on my shoulder.

I pulled away and pointed at Ros and Guil, then at myself and Guts. I scissored my fingers, the sign for walking.

"Yaaa," said Ros, nodding his head.

Martin Luther King he wasn't. But at least he could articulate actual words. Coached by me, Cyrano de Bergerac–style, that might be enough. With practice, he'd improve.

I had a dream . . . or I would if zombies slept.

WITH THE ADDITION of Ros and Guil, we became a true hunting party—three men and a boy. And there was no better place to stalk humans than in their natural habitat.

The question was: Wal-Mart or the mall?

That's the brilliance of *Dawn of the Dead,* the second movie in Romero's trilogy. Set in a shopping center, the film exposes the rib cage of capitalism. Humans are safe within the confines of their shiny prison. They try on furs and fine jewels; they run through the stores, "shopping" with abandon. But it only lasts so long. Because the accumulation of material goods is a panacea, a substitute—it can never fill the void at our spiritual center. It can never acquire the depth of real meaning. It keeps us tethered to the material world, with zombies clawing at the double doors, greedy for more.

And zombies are never satisfied.

Neither are Winona Ryder, Donald Trump, or Jane Doe with her credit card debt of fifteen thousand bucks spent on manicures and pedicures and shoes she'll never wear to glamorous parties she'll only read about in *Glamour* magazine.

I'd rather crave brains than Gucci, Pucci, or Coach. There's an innocence to brains; the desire is instinctual and primitive. Brains are necessary; we need them like sharks need surfers, like babies need mother's milk. And like with babies, our wants are our needs.

Brains are truth. Truth brains. That is all ye know on earth, and all ye need to know.

That's Zombie John Keats, by the way. A pale flower, Keats died at twenty-six after a year of coughing up blood. The way I feel right now, I'd suck on his tubercular handkerchief. The blood of genius.

WE FOUND A Wal-Mart first. Of course. Discount scourge of the nation. It was off I-39 on a commercial strip with Mickey D's, Subway, BK, DQ, KFC, all the acronyms. But there was no grease smell hanging thick in the air; there were no cars snaking through the drive-thrus. The sky was cloudless and Windex blue and it seemed like a late-summer's day, although I can no longer gauge temperature accurately. In fact, I barely feel temperature. I exist; I am that I am. But for the warm tingle at my bite site and my hunger, I'd be as indifferent as a daisy.

A legless zombie was dragging herself down the yellow line in the middle of the road, her torso torn up like ground beef. Other zombies slipped in the trail she left behind.

Members of my tribe surrounded the Wal-Mart, pressing their foreheads against the barricaded automatic doors, leaving streaks of blood on the panes, trying to get to the humans inside. We could feel them in there, going about their business: eating kettle corn and tuna fish, riding bikes, trying on cheap lingerie, making desperate love in the dressing room, shooting guns at targets. And filling the toilets with their waste.

I'm glad zombies don't shit. It gives us a superior moral edge. We don't need Charmin or enemas. We're beyond the body. Beyond good and evil, we use all that we consume; perfectly efficient machines, we absorb nourishment like tapeworms.

With the weight of all those ghouls, eventually the glass Wal-Mart doors would break and zombies would rush in.

I didn't have that long, however; I had to get back to Eve.

The four of us skirted the perimeter of the parking lot and found the back entrance where the oil and lube center was located. There were no zombies back there—just Dumpsters, trucks, wooden pallets, and shopping carts. We waited for humans to come. And come they would, seeking refuge, adult diapers, and Cheez Doodles. Seeking community, lawn chairs, and Milky Way bars. Comfort, trash bags, and Goldfish crackers.

We hid behind a clump of decorative bushes at the edge of the lot. Guts was tending to Guil's neck, wrapping it with what looked like poison ivy. I pointed at the two soldiers and made an inclusive circle with my arms, asking them to join Zombie Army.

"Ahhh," said Ros. "You can . . . count . . . on me."

I threw my fist in the air—power to the undead!—and heard a human squeal. A girl's peal of laughter. My shoulder tingled. I put my finger to my lips and motioned for everyone to crouch down.

"Annabelle," a man said, "be quiet."

"And don't run ahead," a woman said.

"It's okay, Grams. I can shoot a zombie a mile away."

They were less than fifty yards from us, emerging from some trees to cross the parking lot. The girl—a teenager—sported long blond pigtails, a crossbow draped over her Strawberry Shortcake baby tee, and guns stuck in the waist of her low-rise jeans. The old couple clutched each other, their heads whipping from side to side. They appeared to be unarmed.

And oh! How thin the grandparents were! Emaciated as cancer patients. Shuffling on the asphalt in orthopedic shoes. The woman with long white hair coming out of her bun and an eggplant-colored polyester pantsuit; the man bald and bespectacled in a plaid shirt, cardigan, and jeans.

They were poster children for the old and fearful. A commercial for Celebrex.

They would be easy to overpower; the girl was another matter.

"I hope they let us in," the woman said.

"Grandma, that's like the fiftieth time you've said that in the last hour."

"But what if they don't hear us? What if there are zombies?"

"Grandma, there *are* zombies. That's the way it is now. Like the Internet. Suddenly there it is and you've got to deal. Even if you are old."

"Don't talk to your grandmother that way, Annie."

"The guy on the radio said this is the place and this is the way to get in. They'll help us, you'll see. It's all good."

Guts and I were restraining Ros and Guil, both of whom were

ready to charge as soon as they caught a whiff of flesh. But without helmets, they risked getting shot in the head by pretty Annabelle. To communicate this idea, I made a gun with my hand and "shot" Guil with it, then shook my head no and knocked on my helmet. Ros nodded and gave me the thumbs-up. I put my arm around Guts and, through a complicated series of hand gestures and facial expressions, indicated that he and I would capture dinner while Ros and Guil stayed put. I thought they understood.

The best laid plans of zombies and men. . .

"Ohhh," Ros said in his burbling rasp.

It was a loud trumpet. Annabelle snapped to attention.

"Did you hear that?"

"Hear what?" Grandpa said.

"Our hearing's not what it used to be, dear. You know that."

"You guys stay right here, okay? I'm gonna go check it out. Whatever you do, don't move!"

Annabelle marched toward us. If Guts and I couldn't control Ros and Guil, we were destined to be shot by a smart-mouthed teenager in combat boots and trendy clothes.

She could have been a student of mine, one of those postfeminists who eschew the label "feminist" although that's exactly what they are. A lifetime ago, one such young lady had written a paper in my freshmen survey claiming that Spenser's *Faerie Queene* was an allegory of cunnilingus. I'd given her an A, even though the course was contemporary American literature.

My shoulder felt like throbbing gristle—the meat by-product, not the industrial noise band.

It was Guts—our urchin, our orphan, our own li'l Webster—who came up with the plan.

His eyes met mine and he flicked them from Ros to Guil, then to Annabelle. His forehead crinkled significantly. He nodded his head at Grandma and Grandpa and smacked his lips—and I understood.

We let go of Ros and Guil at the same time, and the pair went straight for Annabelle.

"Watch out, dear!" cried Grandma and Grandpa.

Oh, poor zombies, trudging along at turtle speed. Annie had plenty of time to pull out her gun, take aim, and shoot Guil in the head. Kablam! Brains everywhere. I was glad it wasn't Ros. We needed his voice.

Meanwhile, Guts darted out on all fours, quick as a ferret, and bit Annabelle on the ankle. She turned and fired as he scuttled, crab-like, to her grandparents, who were still clutching each other in the middle of the parking lot. The bullet glanced off his helmet. Annabelle grabbed her ankle; an egg-sized chunk of flesh was missing and she was bleeding a royal red. I emerged from the bushes, took out my pipe, and rubbed the bowl.

"You shot my friend," Ros gurgled.

Annabelle looked up. "Dude, you can't talk," she said.

"Says who?" Ros said. Annabelle looked at me. I shrugged my shoulders and attempted a grin. A dollop of my cheek fell off at the dimple. Joan would have to repair that when we got back.

We must've been quite a sight for the girl. Me with my tweed jacket and pipe, Guts with his swift dexterity, and Ros with his exposed cranium and miraculous powers of speech. Her face went through a series of emotions: confusion, shock, disbelief, anger. It was like watching an actor practice her craft in workshop.

Finally, she hit determination, lifted her pistol, and aimed it, first at Ros, then at me. Cool as James Bond, I cocked my head, raised one eyebrow, and pointed behind her at Grandma and Grandpa.

"Brains," Ros said. "Yum." And strolled over to dinner.

The old lady was on the ground, Guts crawling on her like a fruit fly on a moldy peach. Grandpa had an arm around Guts's waist, trying to pull him off. Guts sank his teeth into Grandma's chest just as Grandpa pulled hard; the duct tape and embroidery thread gave way and Guts's guts spilled onto Grandma's stomach. Grandpa let go and gagged.

As for me, I was jonesing hard for some of that cannibal action.

"Hey, kid!" Annabelle yelled. "Get off her!"

She started to run to her grandparents, but her ankle gave out. Standing on one leg, she fired at Guts, hitting him in the back, but he was in la-la land, a feeding frenzy, the point of no return.

I wanted to bring Grandpa back to the Garden of Eden alive so that Joan, Eve, and Kapotas could have fresh meat, and I desperately hoped Annabelle would join the ranks of Zombie Army. That meant I had to be careful, play my cards right. Exercise restraint and *NOT EAT EVERYONE IN SIGHT!*

But a little snack first wouldn't hurt anything.

I knelt down and took a bite out of Annabelle's juicy teenage ass. Spitting out the acid-washed denim, I chewed on the fat. Bootylicious.

Annabelle swiveled her torso and butted me in the head with the handle of her pistol. It made a thudding sound on the army helmet. I took another bite and she hit me in the shoulder, the pistol connecting with my Jason-mask shoulder pad.

"Annabelle!" Grandpa yelled, and he turned and ran toward her. He only made it ten feet before he fell down hard, his face kissing the blacktop.

Great gobs of snot were bubbling out of Annabelle's nose; her bottom was bleeding, but her ankle had already clotted and was turning a deep purplish brown. She turned her pistol around so that the business end was staring me in the face. I pointed at my eye, hugged my chest with my arms, and pointed at her—the universal sign for "I love you."

"Well, I hate you, zombie scumbag," she said, her finger on the trigger.

"Hey," Ros yelled, looking up from Grandma, her blood smeared on his chin, "be nice, girlfriend!"

I inserted my finger in Annabelle's gun, as if that could stop the bullet. If it didn't work for the hippies at Kent State, it wouldn't work for me.

Four dead in Ohio. Millions undead all over the place.

"What the fuck is happening?" Annabelle asked. She was crying, hiccupping and barking like a baby seal.

I took out pen and paper and wrote this: *If you can't lick 'em, join 'em.*

"I'd rather die than be one of you," she said.

Too late, I wrote. *Already infected.*

Annie bent down and touched her ankle—the meat pulsated, almost glowed. She turned, ignoring me, and hobbled over to save Grandma, firing away willy-nilly. I admired her grit. She would make a first-rate soldier, even without cognition.

"Uhhhhhhh!" I yelled.

Grandma was lying open, bare, letting it all hang out. Ros and Guts were chowing down, but Guts looked up at the sound of my voice and in a flash our little trouper sprang forward and attacked, flying through the air like Wonder Dog and coming close to biting Annie's tit off. A strip of her Strawberry Shortcake baby tee caught between his teeth and the two fell backward in an awkward cuddle.

Annie hit her head hard on the asphalt and was down for the count.

"One of us?" Ros asked, pointing at the girl, and I nodded.

Guts scrambled off of Annie's chest and ran back to Grandma. He scooped up a handful of the old lady's brains and presented them to me with an exaggerated bow. I stuffed my face with them.

"She'll be sick soon," Ros said, a piece of intestine hanging out of his mouth.

Annabelle turned green and vomited. I moved her head to the side so she wouldn't choke and dragged her to the grass. She curled up like the sweetheart she was. Her ass had clotted just as it should. I stroked her golden pigtails, fighting the urge to bite her face off.

BY THE TIME we finished Grandma, good to the last scrap of rubbery aged meat, Grandpa had regained consciousness and Annabelle was morphing; she was sick and feverish, murmuring Dashboard Confessional lyrics and rolling her head from side to side.

Grandpa's left side wasn't functioning; apparently he'd had a stroke. Which was lucky for us—he was compliant and docile. We tied him up with Dumpstered twine and lined a Wal-Mart shopping cart with flattened cardboard boxes. We did the same for Annabelle and started back to the Garden of Eden with our groceries.

Cavemen returning home with a mastodon and a woman for the clan.

We had to protect our harvest. The living dead have a sixth sense when it comes to fresh meat and although Grandpa wasn't exactly steak tartare, he was at least alive. Annabelle, on the other hand, was already unpalatable: She smelled like spoiled beans, rotten chicken, and that stuff the janitor sprinkles on puke in grade school.

The best plan was to avoid zombies altogether, which, once we reached the front of the superstore, proved impossible. The crowd of corpses pounding at the double doors moved in our direction, noses in the air like prairie dogs. My shoulder twitched, my bite site tingled, and the urge to join them seized me.

We zombies are a collective, a writhing mass: ants carrying pupae across a puddle, bees working a hive, a pack of wild dogs hunting, humans assembling cars in a factory. The impulse to lose one's self in the swarm, to abandon individuality for group identity, is strong.

Flash mobs, soccer hooligans, Nazism.

The greatest good for the greatest number. . .

We couldn't give in to it.

I grabbed Guts by the elbow and positioned his hands on Grandpa's cart. I simulated running and pointed in the direction of the Garden, giving Guts an encouraging push on his back.

"Wait," Ros said, and picked Guts's guts off the ground, sticking them in the waistband of the young zombie's pants. "Now," he warbled. "Run!"

Guts looked up at me; his eyes widened and I again rejoiced. I loved looking in his eyes. They were yellow and full of pus, like all of us, but the light of understanding was in them. I knelt down and hugged him. His raw guts pressed against me. Never in life had I felt that way for a child. In fact, I'd never felt that way at all, not even for Lucy.

Cry your hearts out, ladies, and hand me the tissues while you're at it. I'm watching *Saving Private Ryan, Brian's Song, Love Story,* and *Steel Magnolias* with you. I'm saying good-bye to cynicism and ironic detachment and hello to love. Because this is *important*. This is a matter of life and death.

Or what passes for life and death in postapocalyptic America.

Of course, the apocalypse label adds weight to everything.

Guts watched the approaching horde with longing, but like the good zombie he was, he set his narrow shoulders, thrust out his scabbed jaw, and took off running with our dinner.

"Good kid," Ros gurgled. "Make it?"

I shrugged. Guts turned onto the frontage road and ran down the alley behind Best Buy and Old Navy. He looked small and alone, like a homeless street kid pushing a shopping cart full of marbleized meat, clogged arteries, a worn liver, two shrinking kidneys, and one glorious brain.

I didn't know who to pray to for his safety. Nobody was watching us; everything was permitted. So I prayed to the only god I could count on:

Oh, Jack Barnes, who art myself, please allow Guts safe passage to the Garden of Eden with our meat alive and intact. This is a world without end. Amen.

ROS AND I took turns pushing the feverish Annabelle up I-39. We saw no humans along the way and the zombies left us alone. They were as clueless as chickens, stumbling pea-brained through cornfields, hay bales, and fences. One zombie walked into a tree and became stuck with his face pressed against the bark, unable to negotiate the obstacle, like a wind-up toy against a wall.

The undead don't avoid bodies of water like the living do. We walk right in, navigating the bottom like catfish, shuffling over the sand and rocks and getting snagged on broken bottles and lost lures. I watched one enter a stock pond, disappear, then reemerge on the opposite bank like the Creature from the Black Lagoon. As miraculous as Chauncey Gardiner.

I felt the urge to preach: "Stop your wandering, my zombie children, and follow me to the Promised Land. The second coming has arrived. The Undead Diaspora is reunited and your suffering has not been in vain. Join us! Together we will meet our maker and fight for a homeland."

"Waaaaaah," is what I said. And they ignored me.

I prayed Saint Joan would save a few pieces of Grandpa for me and Ros. Like Napoleon, I knew that an army marches on its stomach.

If Jesus fed the five thousand with two lousy fish, why couldn't I do the same with one old man?

The truth is, people long for miracles. They want to believe.

"Brains," Ros mumbled. "I like brains." He reached down and petted Annabelle. "One of us," he said. "Soon."

"Worms in my mouth," Annabelle said, slapping at Ros's hand. "Two tons of concrete. Billy, get off me!"

We approached a billboard advertising the Garden of Eden. Take the next exit, the sign said, and turn right. Paradise is one mile down the road, behind the BP. At our pitifully slow pace, it could take us several hours, but I wasn't tired, not in the least. Although we are incapable of rapid locomotion, the walking dead don't need to rest. We can shuffle along forever, circling the globe a hundred times, under oceans, over tundra, crossing deserts.

Except for Guts. He could run. And I can write; Joan could heal and Ros could talk. Blessed are we, the new race, each of us granted one amazing ability. Separately, we are incomplete. Working together, we form a whole.

To paraphrase the Bible, the Gospel according to John: A living grain of wheat remains alone, a single seed; but when it falls into the earth and dies, it bears much fruit.

I looked at Annabelle, who was delirious with fever, covered with vomit, and all-around sick as shit. Ros was pushing her cart, humming the theme song from *Batman*. I prayed Annabelle would be reborn as a Super Friend, with a superpower like us. Another mutant, another adaptation. The X-Men, Magneto and Wolverine. Masters of the Universe and the Powerpuff Girls. Spider-Man, Plastic Man, and Baby Plas. The Green Lantern. O mighty Isis!

Odds were against her—they were against all of us—but I had faith. And if faith can move mountains, then keeping Annie smart would be a piece of cake.

We slogged on down the highway; I thought of Joseph Campbell's *The Power of Myth* and I was comforted. I know heroes exist because I am one. Destiny, fate, Power Rangers, gods, they all exist.

Zombie John Keats called the physical world the valley of soul-making, and I finally understood what he meant. Because I was walking through that valley. I felt it in my brain stem, my cortex, my goddamn pineal gland. He meant transcendence; he meant immortality.

I believe in you, my soul. Through my earthly trials I am creating you.

Holy blade of grass, Batman! Holy plateful of guts.

CHAPTER TWELVE

AS WE NEARED the chain-saw sculpture garden, we heard an ancient narrative unfolding: the childbearing wails of Eve. The birth of Isaac.

"Ooooh," Ros said. "Nasty."

I patted my pretend-pregnant belly, spread my knees, and guided a phantom baby out of my crotch.

"Baby," Ros said. "Zombie?"

I nodded. Ros cooed.

When we entered the Garden, Kapotas was sitting with his back leaning against the Tree of Knowledge, munching on Grandpa's forearm. He turned and hunched over the limb when he saw us, protecting his prize, a dog with his bone. Joan had been busy: There was a boot attached to a short length of broomstick where his foot used to be.

The screen door slammed. Guts ran out and threw his arms around me, pressing his cheek against my belt. He took my hand and led me into the house.

Eve was on the living room floor, legs spread, knees high. Maternity jumper bunched around her waist. Joan sat on the love seat, nurse's hat askew, ripping a sheet into strips. There was a large pile of sheet strips on the cushion next to her, as if she'd been at it for hours, caught in some loop. She stopped for a moment and blew me a kiss, the minx.

It smelled like burning tires and burnt hair. A burnt-out toaster coil and burnt toast. The New Jersey Turnpike on a humid summer day. It smelled like sucking on a battery.

It smelled like zombies.

Kapotas's living room was a cornucopia of Americana: porcelain angels, lace doilies, an afghan over the couch, family photos on every surface, "Footprints in the Sand" on the wall, *Reader's Digest* on the coffee table, and a giant television presiding over it all like a judge.

I knelt next to Eve. She was a wild animal trapped in this bourgeois cage—there was no rationality left in her eyes, just fear.

"When you see only one set of footprints," the Lord says in that famous poem, "it was then that I carried you."

Joan appeared to be out of commission. It was up to me to deliver our child.

Ros popped his head in the door.

"Annie," he said. "Dead. Maybe."

Joan fluttered her hand to her bosom; her mouth opened in surprise at the talking zombie. She rubbed her knee. I motioned for her to attend to Annie and she did as she was told. A teakettle whistled. Guts ran into the kitchen and brought back a pan of hot water and towels.

Towels! Water! What was this, 1956? And what were we, human?

Reference Thomas Kuhn's *Structure of Scientific Revolutions*. There has been a seismic paradigm shift. Like when humans realized the earth is not flat but round, and that it circles the sun, not the other way around. Or when Crick and Watson cracked the DNA code and our genetic secrets were revealed. Or when lonely Pluto got kicked out of the planet club.

If death had finally, finally been conquered, how could babies be delivered in the time-honored way?

I peered between Eve's legs. She wasn't dilated in the least, her pubic hair was crawling with crabs, and a small brown cockroach was perched on her thigh. Isaac's palms pressed against her pelvis, his fingernails scratching to get out.

I snatched up the roach and ate it; the shell crunched like popcorn and its antennae tickled the roof of my mouth. It tasted bland, like puffed rice.

If I didn't get that baby out soon, he'd punch a big hole in his mama, right through her stomach. A mess for Joan to sew back up.

I made a cutting motion. Guts's eyes bugged out and he shook his head.

Eve thrashed on the garish Turkish rug, which was an arabesque of magenta, black, and gold. I made the cutting motion again, this time with a stern look on my rotten face, and Guts ran to the kitchen. Eve grabbed at the end table and pulled on its doily. A picture of Kapotas on his wedding day came tumbling down.

He and his bride were cutting the cake. It looked like the 1970s—Kapotas had muttonchops and a powder-blue tuxedo with ruffles; his wife's long black hair was ironed straight and parted down the middle; her wedding dress was a miniskirt.

Oh, the signs that delineate our decades! Our cultural symbols and codes: Beehives and housedresses. Duck tails and bowling shirts. Handlebar mustaches and corsets. Fringed suede boots and tie-dyed T-shirts. Chaps, holsters, and cap guns.

Pop culture and fashion, the British Romantics and deconstruction—it was all I had in life and I clung to it like religion. It used to be enough, but it meant nothing to me now. Dust in the wind.

Like Charlie Manson said: Now is the only thing that's real.

When Guts returned—scissors and butcher knife in hand—I bent over the prostrate Eve. If I had any breath, I would've held it.

Guts handed me the scissors and I held them poised over Eve's abdomen. Ros sauntered back in and began to sing-croak: "*Clowns to the left of me; jokers to the right. Here I am, stuck in the middle with you.*"

Reference *Reservoir Dogs*. The ear-cutting torture scene. Ros was smarter than he looked. Too bad it sounded like he was at the bottom of a well. Like Baby Jessica, but singing, not sobbing.

I made a tiny cut at the bottom of Eve's beach ball of a belly, stuck my pointer finger in, and wiggled it.

Isaac grabbed it with his fist. Grabbed it tight and pulled. He was a strong baby, a regular monster. My finger came off.

I only had nine digits left—at least until Joan could put me back together again. If she was all the king's horses and all the king's men, then I was Humpty Dumpty. All of us, cracked carnivorous eggs.

I pulled my finger out and looked at the stump. Ros put his hand over his mouth and stifled a giggle. I shook my fist at him à la Ralph Kramden: One of these days, Alice. Pow! Right in the kisser.

Guts scampered to the kitchen and came back with a pair of barbecue tongs.

"Nurse," Ros said, and I nodded. We would need Joan after all.

Oh, the stench of that birth. A million midnight farts underneath the covers. A fish kill, catfish and musky and gar washed ashore, bellies gleaming in the sun-sparkled shallows.

Joan led Annabelle into the delivery room. What a glorious name, recalling Poe's dead maiden in her tomb by the ocean:

And neither the angels in heaven above,
Nor the demons down under the sea,
Can ever dissever my soul from the soul
Of the beautiful Annabel Lee.

She stood erect in the corner, as if waiting for a military inspection. She was still armed, the crossbow draped over her shoulder, guns tucked on either side of her pink rhinestone Hello Kitty belt buckle. I was afraid to meet her eyes, afraid that if I rapped on the metaphorical windows to her soul, no one would answer.

I left the writhing Eve and approached cautiously. Annie lowered her head like a nervous schoolgirl. I put my hands on her shoulders and grunted as gently as possible. She peered up at me through long lashes, and I became a father for the first time that day. Because someone was home. Our Annie was alive. I kissed her once on each cheek, welcoming her to the fold.

"One of us!" Ros said, and jumped up and down, his fringe of golden hair bouncing. He had a mock friar's haircut, a perfect bowl shape, only the top wasn't bald but gone completely. So empty a yarmulke would have fallen right in.

"Aaaaaiii," said Annie, nodding.

"OOOOOH! AAHMMPPH!" cried Eve.

I took off my tweed jacket, picked up the tongs, and turned my attention back to Eve. I rolled up my shirt sleeves—figuratively. Literally, the sleeves were in tatters. Joan was next to me, hot towel at the ready. Guts positioned himself on the other side of the young mother, caressing her bite site with his finger, which was no bigger than a baby carrot. Eve flailed and her stump whacked me in the chin. I looked up at the ceiling and said a silent prayer before plunging the utensils in.

Feeling around in her insides, I grabbed hold of something solid and pulled it out.

In the Zombie Apocalypse, it's always opposite day. Afterbirth is prebirth. Death is life. I put the placenta on the Turkish rug and sat back on my heels. It looked like a giant grape jellybean.

Ros picked it up and smelled it. "Blech," he said. "Sour."

Wasting no time, Joan tugged hard on the umbilical cord. And Isaac tumbled out of the slit in Eve's belly, rolling over and landing bottoms-up at my knees.

I turned the infant over.

"A boy!" Ros said.

Joan handed me the towel. Isaac was covered in muck—dried blood and crusty pus, bits of sunflower yellow and mustard yellow and dead-grass yellow; army green and lime green and forest green and booger green. I picked him up and wiped him off.

He was a big baby—the size of a yearling—and hairless as they come; the whites of his eyes were red; already he had teeth and they were sharp. His tiny nails were pointed.

He was a devil baby. Our zomboy. No wonder the military had wanted to examine Eve. Isaac's prenatal development was unprecedented. A marvel.

I stood up and held him aloft for all to see. Surrounded by my family—Saint Joan, Guts, Ros, Annie, and Eve at my feet—I felt lucky, soulful, alive. On the front lawn, Kapotas shuffled into the birdbath, knocking it over.

The baby cried and I cradled him in my arms. From my Dockers pocket I took out a brain bit and fed him. He ate it in one gulp. Like all newborns, he was ravenous.

CHAPTER THIRTEEN

MY FEAR: WHAT if Isaac doesn't grow?

My other fear: What if he does?

Logic said he would only decay, but logic had been thrown out the window, along with death, taxes, and the social contract. The Age of Reason was long over. Defying modern medicine, Isaac became massive in the womb. Against all likelihood, Annie escaped the dull fate of our brothers. We were in uncharted territory, and without certainties, without a map, I wasn't sure how to proceed.

Sigh. I felt like a teenage goth mall rat stuck in a middle-aged zombie body. A survival plan was not going to emerge from the ether; no Hollywood hero was coming to save the day, no tablets from Mount Sinai to teach us how to behave.

I was a future ancient. A post-culture primitive. None of the zombie movies or the Max Brooks and Dr. Phil books could help me. La Chupacabra, Hook Man, the Man with the Golden Arm, Satan, Ed Gein, Dracula—they couldn't help me.

We were alone. My barbaric yawp fell on deaf ears.

My greatest fear: The moral right is on the humans' side. In the history books, assuming there's a future, zombies will be portrayed as the enemy, the terrorists. The mujahideen and the Janjaweed.

But we only want to survive. We are only obeying our biological imperative.

On the second floor of Kapotas's house, thumbtacked to the walls of his study, were postcards and letters from around the world, all of them thanking Kapotas for creating the chain-saw Garden of Eden. The sculptures touched us, the people wrote. They renewed our faith in Jesus Christ. Thank you, they scribbled, *danke schön, gracias,* for creating such an inspired masterpiece.

Those shortsighted fools. What good does it do now? What is the function of art in the apocalypse? Of religion?

Looking out the window, I watched Guts play with Isaac, trying to teach the zombaby how to run. So far Isaac hadn't grown a whit and he was not a quick study. His chubby legs whirled in an imitation of Guts, his long spiked toenails clicking on the concrete, but when he fell down, he didn't pick himself back up.

Leaves swirled around the two boys. Autumn in the Midwest. Unbroken by clouds, the sky was the color of a frozen corpse.

As soon as I could get everyone stitched up, trained, and stocked with essentials, we'd head for Chicago. Once we demonstrated our sentience to Stein and the other authorities, they'd grant us our civil rights, agree to a compromise. They'd have no choice; we'd eat them if they refused.

AT THIS POINT, get out of your chair, bed, or beanbag; if you're outside, go inside; if you're on the beach, insert your ear-buds and shuffle your iPod. Put on some inspiring music. The theme from *Rocky* would work, or some house or techno, anything with uplifting horns, a rousing beat, and no vocals.

What follows is a montage:

A maple leaf dropping from an almost bare tree. It catches in a wind eddy, circles in a vortex, then wafts to the ground.

Saint Joan fastening a metal plate to Ros's head with screws and hinges; Ros knocking on it to demonstrate its durability.

Guts and Isaac running through the Garden of Eden, Isaac

hiding behind the Ten Commandments. Guts finding him and picking him up, swinging our zomboy in a joyful circle.

Annie shooting her gun at a scarecrow—and hitting the head or the heart every time. Ros at her side, giving the thumbs-up, his metal head reflecting the sun.

All of us hunched over a human, tearing her limb from limb, then retreating to our separate corners to gnaw on the bones, savor the viscera.

Me sitting at a desk in Kapotas's office, pen in hand, surrounded by reference books, composing the document that would save us.

Ros turning on the TV—nothing but static on every station.

Joan, Ros, Annie, and I ransacking the Kapotases' closets and drawers for clothes; Annie trying on vintage 1970s hip-huggers, me a double-breasted suit too short in the sleeves and legs.

Joan and I removing Eve's filthy maternity jumper and dressing her in a navy-blue velour sweat suit. It's like dressing a baby.

Kapotas and Eve drooling, doing the zombie shuffle, walking into totem poles. Guts holding Isaac out for Eve and Eve marching right on by, not even seeing her son.

Pitch-black night, and Ros, Annie, and I lying on our backs with our heads touching, pointing at the constellations.

All of us gathered in the living room, sitting on the embroidered chairs and colonial couch, Ros standing in the center, talking and gesturing, telling the story of our future, our liberty and success.

Me fiddling with the radio. Over the montage music you can hear preachers shouting "rapture," "end times," "sinner," and dragging the Lord's name out to two syllables: law-word.

Pan out the window: The trees are bare, snow is falling. It's winter.

IN HONOR OF the weather, Ros put on a Christmas album and he, Joan, and Annie danced to "Jingle Bell Rock." Oh, what graceless zombies, dancing St. Vitus's dance, delirium tremens, worse than Day of the Dead skeletons or tripping hippies.

I surveyed the troops from a rocking chair: Joan had cleaned her nurse's uniform and was wearing it, although she'd discarded the stockings; her yellow legs were bare except for the suede patch at her knee, but she looked tough enough for the long march ahead.

Soldier-boy Ros was dressed for war with his combat boots, flak jacket, bulletproof vest, and metal head.

And Annie, cute as an undead button in her 1970s jeans and matching vest, her teenage body still nubile—she hadn't been shot yet and had only been bitten three times—Annie was shaking her ass like there was no tomorrow. The pants sagged where the bottom half of her cheek should have been.

Guts whirled in like the Tasmanian Devil. He tossed Isaac on the couch and turned a cartwheel, raring to go.

If Chicago was a bust, if the meeting with Stein turned ugly and my treatise was dismissed, we would continue north. The best way to stave off decay is to stay dry. Ask any Egyptian mummy or frozen Neanderthal. Our choices were desert or tundra. Like Frankenstein's creature, I chose the cold.

We could prolong our living death that way; we might even approach immortality. Assuming we survived the battle.

ONE LAST RADIO scan before we left: "Comfortably Numb" was still playing on DJ Smoke-a-J's station. It'd been on repeat since he was eaten one windy fall day. His demise was broadcast live; we all gathered round the radio like they had in the 1940s, listening.

"They're at the gates," DJ Smoke had said. "The monsters are at the gates! I'm surrounded. Hello, is there anybody out there? Can anybody hear me? If you're listening, if there are any humans left, I just wanna say . . ." He paused and took a shaky breath. "Aw, fuck it. It's for the best, actually. Humanity pretty much sucked, didn't it? Yeah. War, greed, murder, genocide, rape, starvation, child molestation, envy, sloth . . . all those deadly sins from that Brad Pitt movie. Spoiler alert: That's Gwyneth Paltrow's head in the box! Hell, Hollywood's tame compared to reality.

"I'ma go open the doors. Why not let the demons in? At least I know them—they're my neighbors, my family, even my boss is out there. Like it or not, those zombies are us, our true selves. The veil has been stripped away and underneath we are cannibals. Fine Young Cannibals. I never liked that band.

"And those are my parting words in this life—an unsupported opinion of a band no one's cared about since 1990. How banal and trivial. How fitting.

"Here goes nothing. Bye-bye, cruel world."

"Comfortably Numb" came on, doomed to repeat for eternity—or until the signal is interrupted, whichever comes first. DJ Smoke left the mic on, and underneath the strains of Pink Floyd, we heard his screams, along with the slurps, rips, moans, and gurgles of a feed. It made us envious and greedy, gluttonous and lustful.

For brains. Whine it, scream it, say it with need, sarcasm, in a cuddly voice, in the voice of Vincent Price, the voice of Scooby-Doo—any way you slice it, any adverb you attach to it, it remains brains. The object of my desire.

Ros walked into the garage, singing: "There is no pain, you are a zombie. A distant ship, Smoke eaten by zombies."

He was as tuneful as a corpse. I cocked an eyebrow at him.

"Ready to go, captain," he croaked. "Nurse and Annie, check. Two little boys, check. Tweedledee and Tweedledum, secure, leashed, docile."

Ros's speech had improved in our time at the Garden of Eden. I still don't know how he pushed air through his diaphragm, but then again I don't know how I became a brain-crazed, constipated, self-aware zombie either.

We've all got our mysteries.

It's the age-old philosophical question: Why zombies? Or, rather, why not not zombies? Why not nothingness? Why is there something instead of nothing?

I turned the dial. Squawks and screeches. I tuned in to the government station.

It was the same old speech we'd heard a million times: Arm yourselves, vigilantes, martial law, shoot 'em in the head and burn 'em. Another endless loop. Hamster wheels in hamster wheels.

Ros picked up the mic and spoke into it. "Attention," he said. "I am a zombie. Who can talk. There is a group of us and we are heading for Chicago. Smart zombies, if you hear this, go north. We'll find you. Over and out."

He put down the mic. "Think that got out?" he asked.

I shrugged.

"Help some, maybe."

According to Kapotas's AAA maps, Chicago was a little over eighty miles to the east. There were six inches of snow on the ground and more coming down, but we'd make it. We left Paradise at nightfall, determined to gain our rightful place in the world.

CHAPTER FOURTEEN

PICTURE AN AERIAL view, white everywhere, as thick as television snow. The moon is distant and cold, and the stars are sharp as daggers. A small posse of ragtag zombies appears on the left of the scene, trudging to the right. They are a smudge of dirt in the pristine white, a speck of dark in the light. Climbers on Everest. Ring around the collar.

Zoom in: Ros, Annie, Joan, Guts, and I form the nucleus; Kapotas and Eve are attached by ropes, circling us like electrons or tentacles; and Guts is pulling Isaac on a red plastic Wal-Mart sled.

We are a rainbow of decay: Khmer Rouge red, Baghdad blue, gangrene green, bruised-apple brown.

We were shuffling down State Highway 72, a two-lane road running parallel with I-90. Motorcycle helmets, shopping carts, and Converse All-Stars. An Amish carriage lay on its side, the door open and its dark interior exposed.

It was as silent as the beginning of the world.

And in the beginning was the word and the word was brains.

Ros began to sing "Silent Night."

Annie joined in: "Arrrooomphaugh," she sang.

I put my arm around her. "Oooaaampher," I gurgled.

Joan, Guts, and Isaac raised their voices too—even Kapotas and Eve. We sang to the darkened sky. A chorus of moans and bleats and bubbling vowels, howling at the moon. A pack of wild dogs answered from across the prairie.

God was blessing us. God is blessing us every one.

WE WALKED ALL night, and in the morning we sat on top of a station wagon like turtles lined up on a log, watching the sunrise.

Zombies have at least one distinct advantage over the living: We're as sensitive as frogs, awake to subtle chemical changes in the atmosphere. It's an adaptation that counterbalances our many failures in communication and mobility, and aids immeasurably in the hunt.

That's how we knew there was a group of humans at least a mile off. They were hurrying toward us, headed west and away from Chicago. Their aroma preceded them.

The core group—Ros, Joan, Annie, Guts, and I—lumbered off the car and closed ranks. Eve and Kapotas began to move forward, pulling on the ropes like rabid dogs.

"Hooray!" Ros said. "Breakfast."

I counted with my fingers.

"How many?" Ros said. "Good question."

Annie released the safeties on her weapons, Ros tightened his bulletproof vest, and Joan knelt down to mother Guts, adjusting his helmet and straightening his clothes.

But there were only five of us—seven if you counted Eve and Kapotas. And I didn't. They'd be useless in a real battle. Nothing more than cannon fodder.

Ros raised his fist. "Charge!" he said.

I grabbed his shoulder. There weren't enough helmets to go around and Ros's metal head, while it offered some protection, wasn't bulletproof. If we charged, we'd lose.

I looked around for a place to hide, figuring we could lie in wait for the humans, see how many there were, what weapons they carried, and then ambush them . . . or not.

There was a structure up the road. I pointed to it and crouched down, twisting my neck to the left and right, pretending to be a hunter in a deer stand.

"Got it," Ros said. "Recon."

We scuffled toward the structure. Eve's mouth twitched in an approximation of a smile; she understood we were heading for meat. I gave Guts a push on his bony back. He handed Isaac's rope to me and zoomed ahead.

It was a homemade fruit stand, pieced together with cheap two-by-fours. Nails hadn't been hammered in straight and stuck out at odd angles. The lumber was rotting, the wood flaking and peeling in spots, and there were empty fruit crates scattered around. A hand-lettered sign out front read FRIED PIES.

By the time the rest of us reached it, Guts was already inside, rooting around in the trash. He found a Matchbox car—a fire engine covered with dirt—and *vroomed* it on the snow. Ros creaked down and sat cross-legged next to the imp, playing make-believe with him.

"Next is hide-and-seek," Ros said. "Understand?"

Guts rolled his truck up and down Ros's arm and nodded.

I parked Isaac behind the fruit stand and herded the rest there as well, then trundled around to the front to check out the view. It was important that no one be visible from the road.

No such luck. Eve and Kapotas would not stay put. Their arms extended beyond the boundaries of our fort, reaching out for the humans like fans seeking autographs from the biggest pop star in the world.

The feeling in my shoulder intensified. Our quarry was getting close. "Ooormph," I cried, and somehow Joan understood. She pulled on the ropes and the dumb duo fell backward behind the stand. I walked as quickly as I could to safety. Eve and Kapotas would have to be restrained as the humans walked by. I hoped we could restrain ourselves.

I re-created the battleground by scratching our position in the snow with a stick. I depicted us hiding behind the fruit stand and the humans moving toward it. I drew lines between us and them like a coach diagramming football plays.

I looked to Ros for a recommendation. Even though I was the

leader, Ros was a soldier, experienced in warfare. His input was indispensable. I pressed the stick into his hand.

"Annie here," he said, indicating that she should position her gun on top of the counter. "Wait until they pass us by. Then shoot. Back-door attack."

It was a good plan. We wouldn't get them all, but we didn't need them all. Just one or two would do. I gave my helmet to Annie—with her head above the counter, she would be the most vulnerable.

"Everyone shh," Ros said. "Here they come."

The humans entered our field of vision. There were seven of them, walking in loose formation and at a pace I envied. Only one of them appeared to be armed, a bulky man in an orange hunting cap. A girl about Guts's age pulled an infant on a sled.

Eve started moaning. I made a zip-your-lip motion with my hand and Joan covered Eve's mouth with a handkerchief. I was holding tight to Kapotas; Ros cuddled Guts in his lap.

The little band of humans passed our hideout, the gunman so close I could hear him muttering under his breath. Every dead cell in my body was screaming to be fed, but I didn't move. None of us did.

"Quiet out here," one of the people said.

"We haven't seen any zombies for miles," a woman said. "Maybe they're mostly in the cities?"

"Haven't seen any people either," said the man I took to be their leader. Like me, he had tortoiseshell glasses. Unlike me, he was bundled up in a parka and ski mask, protecting his fragile skin from the cold. That's another advantage we zombies have: We're impervious, some might say oblivious.

Then I was looking at his back, and that could have been the end of it. We could have let them pass unharmed. They'd never know we were there, never know how close they'd come to death.

If only they didn't taste so good.

Ros nudged Annie with his elbow. She stood up, took aim, and blasted the gun-toting traveler in his shoulder blade. The gun flew out of his hand and slid across the icy snow.

The group turned to face us. They went on the defense, vigilant and tense, raising their shovels and baseball bats. Pitiful weapons. The young girl pulled the sled closer and picked up the baby.

"Don't shoot!" the leader said. "Can't you see we're human?"

Annie shot him in the stomach. He bent over and collapsed, his blood turning the snow into the most delicious of sno-cones.

Guts scurried out from behind our shelter, retrieved the gun, and pounced on the slain gunman; the rest of us stood up and began our laborious attack. The humans gasped collectively.

They were our parallel-universe doppelgangers, right down to the teenager and baby. It was like looking in a funhouse mirror, our bizarro-world selves. We stared at each other for a moment, taking the coincidence in.

"You have brains," Ros said.

Well put, I thought. I couldn't have said it better myself.

"Run!" the fallen leader yelled, his hand clutching his abdomen.

The spell was broken. They took off, except the brave one who stayed behind to help the leader, offering her body as support so they could hobble to their deaths together.

"I'm as good as dead," the man said to her. "Save yourself."

She stood up, unsure, watching Joan, Ros, and me walking toward her.

"Annie," Ros said, pointing to the woman. "Shoot her."

But Annie was behind us. She couldn't get off a decent shot. We were in the way.

Meanwhile Eve and Kapotas reached the gunman and commenced feeding. Their crunching and moaning was loud and rude. The woman turned her head at the sound, her mouth opened in a silent scream.

"Go!" the leader yelled.

She turned and ran, zigzagging to make herself a moving target. Annie shot and missed by an inch; snow flew upward where the bullet buried itself.

We reached the leader and snapped our jaws at him. To his credit, he put up a fight, smashing snow in my face and kicking Joan in the groin. Too bad for him, his attempts were futile, like a bunny trying to escape the mouth of a cat.

Ros unbuttoned the man's parka and lifted up his sweater and thermal shirt, peeling the layers like an onion. He took a bite of his stomach and made a face.

"Tastes like lead," he said.

I shrugged. That's what happens when you shoot your prey. I bit into the man's shoulder. It was delectable, not a trace of bullet residue. His blood bloomed like roses on the snow.

WE MARCHED FOR a thousand more years. For a long stretch, Illinois was desolate. The trees were weighted down with ice, limbs luminous in the low winter sun. Once the snow stopped, it was dry and crisp, frost crunching underfoot and ice chunks falling from power lines. The highway was slippery and we fell often, sometimes dragging Kapotas and Eve when they couldn't—or wouldn't—pick themselves back up.

I envied Isaac—he had always been a zombie; he had no memories to haunt him on this endless trek. No human memories, that is.

As for me, I had a million.

Like the moment I fell for Lucy. She was a student in my semiotics class and I'd hardly noticed her until she was tardy one day, slipping in during my lecture on Umberto Eco's seminal text *Travels in Hyperreality*. We were dissecting the essay on Disneyland.

It was my first semester in the Midwest. I was not yet acclimated to the culture and so was surprised to see Lucy wearing Winnie the Pooh pajama bottoms, a sweatshirt emblazoned with the university logo, and dirty suede moccasins. Her hair was long then and pulled into a sloppy ponytail.

"Are you in the habit of wearing your sleepwear to class, Miss?" I asked.

"Ludlow," she said. "And it's Ms."

She found a seat, took out her notebook, which was metallic silver, and her pen, which was metallic pink with a fluffy pink glittery ball on the end. She looked at me attentively, that ridiculous pen poised above the paper.

Lucy had all the hallmarks of the anorexic—immense and sunken eyes, cheekbones like jagged edges, baggy clothes, and skeletal hands. I adored anorexics. With their low self-esteem, desire to please, and rigorous self-discipline, what's not to like?

"Well, Ms. Ludlow?" I said.

"Excuse me?" She blinked.

"I asked if you were in the habit of wearing your pajamas to class." The tips of her ears turned red.

"Is something wrong?" she asked.

"Let's pause for a moment," I said to the class. "Take a brief detour with me while we ponder the semiotic message Ms. Ludlow is sending by wearing her jammies to school. Please, if you don't mind, Ms. Ludlow, could you stand up in front of the class?"

Lucy stood and the dear girl vamped it up. Turning in a circle, her hands on her boyish hips, pointing her toe, she looked like a Sears catalogue model. We all had a laugh and then I led a discussion on the cultural myths and ideologies implicit in wardrobe choices, the ever-changing rules governing fashion and decorum. My students taught me that in the Midwest it's acceptable to wear pajama bottoms to class or the supermarket, even the coffee shop. Philistines, I thought. Can't tell mole from gravy.

The next class period Lucy wore a skirt and blouse, and on our wedding night, she emerged from the bathroom wearing those same Winnie the Pooh bottoms. I pulled them down, turned her over, and gave her a good spanking.

I'll be the first to admit it: I was an asshole.

It took zombiedom to give me a soul, death to make me "human."

Scouting ahead of us, Guts found a corpse at a Kum and Go. Male. From the waist down, he was unharmed and clothed in Levi's and Nikes. He had no torso or head, just a spinal cord sticking straight out of his pelvis, picked clean of every speck of flesh, like a lollipop stick. By his side was a pistol. He must've shot himself and then been eaten by vultures or crows, not zombies. Otherwise his legs would be marching in blind circles.

We fell to our knees and gobbled his groin, thighs, ankles, feet, all of it, the meat tough and old but at least not poisoned with the virus.

Eve was stooped over the body. Her hair had grown, as everyone knows it continues to do after death, and it hung in her eyes. She shoved the guy's bladder in her piehole, rubbing blood over her face like a porn star. She was nothing like my skinny Lucy. Not even close.

AS WE NEARED Chicago, we began to see more zombies. Wandering the shoulder and weaving down the yellow line. Icicles hanging from their noses, their open wounds like Coke slushies, their eyes as filmy as dirty snow. Isaac moaned for fresh meat. My professor pockets were empty.

"Must be cold," Ros kept repeating. "But can't feel it. Hungry, hungry, hunger, hunger, hunger. I'm so well hunger. Ha. Brains. Oh. Where's Sergeant Collins?" He trailed off, mumbling, then began the litany again.

The moon went from full to crescent, slivered like a thumbnail.

We hadn't seen a rabbit or squirrel in days. All creatures great and small, eaten by or hiding from my kinsmen. Only the birds remained, flying out of reach.

With zombies at the top of the food chain, the ecosystem was out of whack. If current trends continued, we'd eat ourselves into extinction.

By the time we reached Cook County, the road was thick with zombies. Like Times Square on New Year's Eve, it was hard to shuffle through them all. So many were naked or wearing only soiled boxer briefs or thongs or their clothes were shredded like shipwreck survivors on a deserted island, their bodies gray and covered with cuts and bruises. Breasts sagged to hipbones. Cocks and balls hung limp as if stricken with some incurable venereal disease. Joan's eyes darted from patient to patient, her doctor's bag clutched in her hand; with her perky cap, she looked like an alert blue jay.

And our hunger. And our moans. We were deafening. Distracting.

It took all of my will to keep our little group focused and together, to fight the urge to join the pack and wander without purpose, lose identity, become just another ant.

I understand why humans join cults. Free will is overrated.

There's freedom in surrender. Ask any POW. Ask any kidnapped kid with Stockholm syndrome. The questions are over: What do you want to do tonight, dear? What do you want for dinner? Should we have kids? Rural, urban, suburb, or exurb? Paper or plastic? Coke or Pepsi?

There are no more questions because there's only one answer left:

Brains. Do I repeat myself? Very well then—I repeat myself. Brains, brains.

Did I mention brains?

Damn, was I hungry.

We had to get off that state highway to hell. Saint Joan was dragging Eve through the snow and Eve was turning into a Popsicle. Eventually the rope tethering them together would cut Joan's arms off and then who'd sew us back together?

I steered us off the road and toward a strip mall with a Dollar Tree, a Rent-A-Center, a Payless, and an empty parking lot covered with virgin snow.

If only I had some capital and a supplier, I could open a Brains Superstore in that strip mall. Good location, plenty of customers. BrainsMart, I'd call it. Or BrainSmart. How about Old Brainy? Brains R Us. I could go on, but why bother?

Beyond the mall was a scrubby little field, and beyond that a scrubby suburb of cookie-cutter McMansions and McTown Houses. That's where we headed. From there, we'd continue east, through fields and subdivisions, away from the highway with its teeming masses. Even if we were to encounter an edible human on the main road, the competition would be keen.

"Hunhhhhhm," Saint Joan gurgled. She was struggling with Eve, trying to lift the insentient Mother Zombie off the snow. There were rust-colored ice crystals hanging off Eve's stump and her entire back was frozen solid like a side of beef hanging on a meat hook. Joan showed me her shoulders; the rope had burned through her nurse's uniform and was making headway into her flesh.

"Stupid zombie," Ros said, pointing at Eve where she lay on the snow. "Stupid zombie," he repeated, pointing at Kapotas, who was at least standing on his own but leaning forward on his peg leg as if about to fall, his arms hanging at his sides. The blue embroidery thread on his neck was unraveling.

Nothing lasts forever. Not even zombies.

I nodded. If I had any breath, I would've exhaled a plume of steam in the cold air.

"Undead weight," Ros said. "Slowing us down."

Guts pelted Ros with a snowball, hitting him on his metal head.

"Why you little . . . ," Ros said, and took off after the rascal.

Poor Ros. Our speedy Gutsy Gonzalez ran circles around him. Because Ros, despite his amazing ability—pull his string and watch him talk!—traveled at zombie speed. Ros stretched his arms out, thumbs together in the classic throttling position—Homer Simpson about to choke Bart—and shuffled a few inches through the snow. Guts hit him with another snowball, square in the face.

Sitting in his red plastic sled, Isaac clapped his devil hands.

Rosebud, I thought. Red wheelbarrow. All of it necessary.

Ros had a point about Kapotas and Eve, but I couldn't abandon the mother of the child. Not yet.

We heard a caw, and a pair of crows flew overhead, dwarfing the snowbirds and cardinals we had been seeing. Annie drew her pistol, aimed, shot twice, and the crows thumped to the ground. Everyone clapped her on the back. Our sharpshooter. Not consumptive Annabel Lee but Annie Oakley, Queen of the Dead Midwest. I pointed at Guts, then in the direction of the felled birds, and he jogged off to fetch them.

"Love that kid," Ros said. He looked at Annie. "You too," he said.

Guts returned with the birds. They were scrawny and underfed, but we ate them, feathers, feet, bones, beaks, eyes—everything. Zombies are like Indians; no part of the animal is wasted.

"Mooooaaaauah," Kapotas moaned, grabbing for the pebble-sized heart speared on Isaac's fingernail. Before he could reach it, however, Guts sprang to action and tackled Kapotas, who went down like a meat mannequin. Guts perched on the sculptor's barrel chest, restraining him while munching on a crow's foot.

"Needs salt," Ros said, iridescent black feathers hanging from his mouth. "And brains."

What a joker he was, a regular Groucho Marx.

After the meal, we headed toward the subdivision. Kapotas remained on the ground and I didn't coax him up. If he rose on his own, we wouldn't prevent him from coming with us; we weren't cruel. But he didn't. He just lolled right where Guts tackled him, staring up at the sun and moaning. Saint Joan looked back at him, and if she were capable of nuanced expression, I'd say her face was wistful. She was, after all, a healer.

"Good riddance," Ros said. "Bad rubbish." He pointed at Eve, who was walking backward, being pulled by me. "Her next."

CHAPTER FIFTEEN

OURS WERE THE only footprints on the snow-covered asphalt, and the trail we left behind was dragging and heavy as if we were skiing, not walking. We passed the subdivision's sentries: two concrete lions atop two concrete pillars with the word KING'S etched in one and COURT in the other.

King's Court was a typical housing development—all the trees had been razed to pour foundations and only a few homeowners had bothered to plant new ones. The houses were a combination of aluminum siding and brick, with a maximum of three floor plans to choose from. There were no sidewalks or corner stores, but there were basketball hoops in driveways, plastic play sets in backyards, and two-car garages. Inside the houses we found Berber and shag carpets, linoleum kitchens with faux-granite countertops, and more bathrooms than necessary.

We wandered up and down Bishop Lane and Queen Street, through Knight's Crossing and Crown Drive, zombies on a giant chessboard of middle-class mediocrity. We ransacked the houses, hoping for a whiff of human or pet and searching for supplies.

In a two-story Tudor on Pawn Way, Joan found an all-terrain stroller for Isaac. It was one of those trendy carriages, a three-wheeler with a Gore-tex awning and shock absorbers. Designed for the active mother trying to lose that baby weight, it used to cost more than a beat-up station wagon. It was free now.

Guts lifted Isaac from his sled and strapped him into the stroller, fussing over the baby like a mother hen.

Although Isaac could walk, he preferred not to and I didn't blame him. Like free will, walking is overrated. Plus, the tot wasn't very good at it, wobbling around like a drunken devil, and we all enjoyed coddling and protecting him.

We believed Isaac was the future.

There was movement at the end of the cul-de-sac, a human scurrying from Rubbermaid trash can to Ford Focus like a wild animal. We picked up the scent, bite sites tingling, and convened in the middle of the street.

Everyone except Eve, that is. She took off after the creature, arms raised, helmet on sideways, the ear protector covering her left eye. Ros was right: Eve was a liability. Her presence did not contribute to our cause; in fact, she undermined our credibility. It was like allowing a convicted rapist to join NOW. I had to face the facts: She was incapable of learning. A mindless sheep.

We let Eve go on her stupid march. With hand gestures and nods we planned our own attack.

"Looks like a child," Ros said. "Feral."

Saint Joan nodded. Guts jumped up and down, clapping his hands and rubbing his duct-taped belly.

That Guts, the pixie, he was no longer black; he no longer bore the cross of his race. Annie, Ros, and Joan were no longer white, and neither was I. In zombiehood, race is erased. Brothers and sisters of the brain, we are gray, the ultimate race, a nation of nations. We are completely homogeneous. As a society we would be quite peaceful; all of the differences we used to fight over—religion, race, oil, the economy—are wiped out. We are a single unit, a focused target audience, a marketer's dream.

If we were five zombies with consciousness, how many more of us existed? One out of every hundred? Out of a thousand? Ten thousand? How many in total? Enough for a revolution, that much I knew.

A gunshot rang out. We looked at Annie; her guns were holstered.

Eve was walking down the street like a crippled cowboy in a western. *The Great Brain Robbery. A Fistful of Viscera. The Quick and the Undead. The Good, the Bad, and the Zombie.* Another few paces and she might turn and shoot, spurs twinkling and jingling.

There was another shot, and this time I heard it ping Eve's helmet. She continued walking, totally unaware.

"Stupid, stupid, stupid zombie," Ros said.

We took cover in a garage. Next to a weed whacker was a pile of dog bones, matted fur still stuck to them. Ros picked up a rib—it had been a big dog, maybe a German shepherd judging from the hair—and gnawed on it. He handed Isaac a piece.

"Reverse situation here," he said. "Me chewing on a dog bone. Like a dog. With his bone." He crunched. "Crazy goddamn world."

I bent down and put my arm around Guts. I poked his tummy, pointed at the wagon in the corner—a classic Red Flyer—then shook my finger, which flopped and wiggled, held on by nothing more than Krazy Glue, at Eve.

"Jesus," Ros said. "Captain wants the kid to save her. Lovestruck fool."

I shook my fist at Ros. He stuck his tongue out at me. It looked like sloughed snake skin.

Saint Joan tightened the helmet straps under Guts's chin. The urchin looked like a Pound Puppy plushie; his eyes were milky and plastic, the lashes caked with dirt and soot in such a way that they separated, appearing lush and long, like Tammy Faye Bakker eyelashes.

I gave him a little push and he was off.

"Suicide mission," Ros said once Guts was out of earshot, halfway down the street, running as fast as he could, the little red wagon wheels squeaking.

Eve didn't even turn at the clatter. In her defense, she only had the one ear. Guts took bullets to his guts, his chest; nothing slowed him down. It was like the Iraq War footage we all saw on television before the zombie outbreak—the intrepid American soldier in the new urban battlefield, executing a daring guerrilla mission, dodging enemy fire, kicking down doors, searching for insurgents.

I suppose that war's over. Guess what? Zombies won.

In no time Guts reached Eve and rammed the wagon into the backs of her knees, causing her to fall into it. He turned and trotted toward us, Eve spilling over the sides of the wagon, her feet and stump scraping the street. The shots stopped.

I imagined triumphant music. "Pomp and Circumstance" or something military. Guts made a victory fist and pumped it in the air. I reimagined the scene in slow motion.

To put the brains on the icing on the cake, the sniper made an error: He poked his head out the window of a three-story brick monstrosity.

We knew exactly where he was. Which house, which window. We knew his ball cap was green and he sported a full, dark beard. The man was trapped in a suburban nightmare. And this was no metaphorical trap like before the epidemic. As in: *Oh! The tragedy of being owned by your possessions! Cry for me because I am rich yet my soul is poor!* Please. This time it was literal. There was no exit.

Of course, everything is literal now. The metaphor is as dead as I am.

And I didn't want to eat Green Cap Sniper. Allow me to rephrase that: I very much wanted to eat Green Cap Sniper. I was horny for his brains. If I was Zombie Verlaine, then he was Rimbaud.

But—and here's the delicate turn, my narrative's volta—he was worth more to us alive.

According to the history books, that's what Che Guevara—revolutionary Christ figure, beret-wearing silkscreen on a thousand T-shirts—that's what he told the CIA before they shot him, before they cut off his hands postmortem. Not that it mattered.

There's nothing new under the sun.

I communicated my plan to the gang, pantomiming the attack on Green Cap, mimicking a feeding, then shaking my head no. Vehemently. Ros agreed.

"Muzzle her," he said, jerking a thumb at Eve, who was still sprawled in the wagon, lowing in the alto range.

I got in the car and acted human. I adjusted my pretend ball cap and put my hands on the steering wheel at six and nine o'clock. Guts hopped in the passenger side. The keys were in the cup holder and I thought, What the heck, maybe we don't need Green Cap. After all I've learned in my new incarnation, maybe I can drive. It was a Crown Victoria, an old person's car, fully automatic, designed to float like a boat and guzzle gas as if the oil supply were endless.

I picked up the keys, located the right one, and tried to fit it in the slot. I jabbed at the ignition a few times, but the task seemed impossible, the level of coordination beyond me. I gave myself a pep talk: You can do it, professor!

Nothing happened. The keys fell out of my hands and slipped underneath the gas pedal. Guts and I just sat there in the garage like two kids playing Sunday Afternoon Drive.

The separation was complete: physical and spiritual; mind and body; thought and action. I was the living dead embodiment of Cartesian dualism: Though my soul was housed in my body, my body was divorced from my soul.

Ros pointed at me and squealed. The sound was otherworldly— a rabid pig with emphysema, a demon gloating over murders and wars, a cannibal with a baby at the end of his spear, Donald Sutherland in the final scene of *Invasion of the Body Snatchers*.

Saint Joan covered her mouth with her hand, hiding her rotten teeth, putrid tongue, and obvious glee at my incompetence.

Humans call it laughing, but zombies don't have a name for it. We don't have a name for anything.

I got out of the car and held the door open for Ros. Let him try it, if he's so smart.

Ros climbed in. And sat there. And continued to sit there. Impotent, like me.

"Can't," he gurgled.

As a human, I would have said something cutting to demonstrate my superiority. But I'm a compassionate zombie. My anger drained away and I was flooded with pity. Our poor dumb species. We'd never make it.

"Joan?" Ros said.

I looked at Joan and she shook her head, waving her hands in a gesture of adamant protest. I walked over to her, intending to escort her to the vehicle, when my shoulder began tingling, and everyone, Annie, Guts, Ros, Joan, even Eve, perked up, alert and poised. Stiff as lawn statuary.

Green Cap Sniper was approaching.

Eve headed straight for the brains, as steadfast as a pimp targeting a runaway. Guts sprang forward and closed the garage door in her face. Eve walked right into it, clawing at the barrier and moaning.

Part of me admired Eve. Her behavior was classic Romero zombie and there's something to be said for tradition. Like a woman who stays home to raise the kids, she was old-school.

"Muzzle her," Ros repeated, and I nodded.

Saint Joan grabbed the garden hose and tied Eve up. She removed Eve's helmet and gave it to Annie. Guts took Isaac out of his stroller and they stood facing the garage door, holding hands.

"Lock and load," Ros said, looking at Annie.

Corn-fed and flaxen-haired Ros's dialogue was straight out of *Die Hard with a Vengeance*. I imagined he was that star quarterback in high school who got drunk on weekends and popped the head cheerleader's cherry, the kid who sailed through algebra and *Beowulf* on his beefy good looks. After graduation, he joined the military to keep America free.

"Don't eat the human," Ros reminded everyone. We were standing in formation, lined up for battle. "Everyone ready?" he said. "Let's roll."

The only thing I rolled was my eyes. If all language is fossil poetry, as Emerson claimed, then Ros was burning fossil fuel faster than a jet engine. Rehashing tired movie clichés, not an original thought in his head.

Annie's gun was drawn and cocked, her finger on the trigger. I nodded at Guts and he opened the garage door.

Green Cap was in the driveway, feet planted a foot apart, rifle drawn in a defensive posture. Isaac crawled toward his legs, but Guts grabbed the devil child by the seat of his onesie. Eve was writhing on the floor, the garden hose coiled around her like a snake. Saint Joan clutched her doctor's bag and moaned, a plaintive wail filled with such longing I almost gave in to desire myself.

"What the fuck," Green Cap said.

Imagine you haven't eaten in a week and your favorite dish—fried chicken or foie gras, beef Wellington or beef tacos—is in front of you. Or you've been crawling across the Sahara for three days, sun pouring down on your bald spot, sand in your teeth and eyes, and you can't even sweat anymore, you're that dry, and the lake in front of you is not a mirage but an oasis.

And you can't eat or drink. Verboten.

"Brains," Ros said. It was the truest thing anyone has ever said.

Green Cap sighted with his rifle but before he could squeeze the trigger, Annie shot it out of his hand.

"Jesus," Green Cap said.

Here I am, I thought, resurrected and full of grace.

Green Cap took a step backward. It was fight-or-flight time, and it looked like he was going to fly.

Ros cleared his throat; it sounded like the glub of the Loch Ness Monster, a creature whose existence I'm currently rethinking. Because if zombies exist, why not Nessie?

"We come in peace," Ros said.

Annie and Joan inched toward Green Cap, each step painfully slow, stroke victims learning to walk again. Annie brandished a rope, lasso-style. Guts tucked Isaac back into his pram.

"Holy Mother of God," Green Cap said, and turned and ran. Guts followed suit, and the chase was on.

What a miracle Guts was. He dove for Green Cap's feet and tackled him before they reached the cul-de-sac.

And poor Guts. Longing illuminated his urchin's face, but he could only sit on top of the human until the rest of us reached them. No biting, no touching, like a lap dance.

Green Cap was thin; he probably hadn't eaten a Hot Pocket in days. He looked like Paul Bunyan. His hair was long and matted underneath the John Deere cap and his beard was wild and woolly. He was wearing jeans, a flannel shirt, a down vest, and Timberland work boots. He was a survivor, all right. Who knew how many of us he'd fought off? Hundreds, at least.

He punched Guts in the face. He wrapped his hands around Guts's neck and choked him, trying to poke his thumbs into our little guy's eyes. Guts bared his teeth, snapping at Green Cap's thumbs.

And one small bite is all it takes. . .

"Don't do it," Ros warned him.

"This can't be happening," Green Cap said. He let go of Guts's neck and propped himself up on his elbows, ignoring the adorable zomboy perched on his chest. He watched us approach. By now, we were halfway down the driveway. "Are you all zombies?" he asked.

"We like brains," Ros admitted.

"Is this really happening?" Green Cap asked.

"You better believe it," Ros said.

"Why are you talking?" Green Cap asked.

"Why are you?"

Green Cap rested his head on the concrete. "Then it's over," he mumbled, "if they can think."

Here's my favorite recipe. Pretend you're reading *Like Water for Chocolate*.

Ingredients: One human, warm and alive, preferably wriggling, maybe screaming.

Preparation: Using both hands, hold human firmly in place. Take a big bite. Chew. To enhance flavor, let pieces of flesh and viscera swing from mouth.

Repeat until human is a pile of bones.

But I couldn't do it. It was triumph-of-the-will time. Mind over matter. Brain over brains.

I had a mantra and it was this: Do not eat the human . . . Do not eat the human . . . Do not eat the human . . . Do not eat. . .

Eve's moans were at a fever pitch, loud enough to attract our brethren. She needed a sock in her maw. Pronto. I signaled as much to Joan, putting my hand over my mouth and nodding in Eve's direction. The old gal did a 180, back to the garage, almost creaking as she turned. She was a dutiful zombie, a first-class minion.

We were almost to the end of the driveway. The Trail of a Thousand Zombie Tears.

"Brains," Ros said. "Mmmmmmm."

Ros's arms were outstretched; he was slipping into character, losing cognition. I grabbed his elbow and shook him. Forcing him to face me, I made the peace sign, then pointed the two fingers to my eyes, then to his eyes, signaling: Look at me. Stay with me.

Do not eat the human . . . Do not eat the human . . . Do not eat the human . . . Do not eat. . .

Saint Joan muffled Eve's moans. The suburb was quiet save for Green Cap's sobbing. No snow shovels hit concrete; no children cried "Ollie ollie oxen free." There were no dogs barking or screen doors slamming or cars revving. No middle-aged women power-walking or Mormons knocking on doors.

No one was left.

We reached Green Cap. Guts jumped off him and helped Annie hog-tie his ankles and wrists together.

"Why are you doing this?" Green Cap asked.

"You drive," Ros said.

"You want me to be your chauffeur?"

We nodded.

"None of you can drive?" he asked.

"Too hard," Ros said.

I took out my pad, wrote this down, and held it in front of Green Cap's eyes:

Dear Sir,

Don't be afraid. Although we covet your brains, we need you to drive us to Chicago. And please, call me Jack.

"Holy shit," Green Cap said, looking up at me.

"Nice man," Ros said. "He'll drive."

Green Cap wiggled on the driveway like a worm. Annie and Guts had done a fine job with the rope. "Don't see that I have a choice," he said. "How many like you are there?"

I shrugged my shoulders.

"We're special," Ros said.

I pointed at the note, like the ghost of Christmas future forcing Ebenezer Scrooge to look at his own grave.

"Okay, Jack," Green Cap said. "You can call me Pete. I used to be an electrician but now I'm a survivor. A good one too. After the evacuation, I ruled all of King's Court." He lifted his chin as if to encompass the entire subdivision.

"Not anymore," Ros said.

Up the street, a flash of color, along with a fresh tingling in my shoulder. The feral. I nodded at Annie and Guts and they took off, Guts running ahead, Annie lagging behind with the rifle over her shoulder.

Saint Joan came walking down the driveway, swinging her doctor's bag and winking like a kind, matronly nurse in a World War I movie.

Compared to the Zombie Apocalypse, World War I was a walk in the park. Forget trench warfare and machine guns. Forget Woodrow Wilson and *A Farewell to Arms*. Hell, forget World War II and Hiroshima while you're at it. Remove genocide and the postwar baby boom from your mind.

Now is the only thing that's real.

"Leave Eve," Ros said.

"Groooaaamph," I said, meaning, "Perhaps."

I wondered if humans still did it, the old in-out. And whether Pete was lonely in his barren subdivision. Were matters of the flesh and heart important to him? Were there Jews left in Israel?

Did the Holy Land ever even exist in the first place?

I wrote Pete another note: *We need to find Howard Stein, creator of the virus. Is he still alive? Take us to him.*

"Stein. Him," Pete said. "Killed by a mob, apparently. Of humans, mind you, not the undead. This is word-of-mouth info— no more CNN—so I can't vouch for the truth of it. But yeah. His own kind turned on him."

"Go on," Ros said, and coughed up some black goop.

"From what I heard," Pete continued, glancing at Ros, "zombies controlled most of the city. A group of scientists and politicians were holed up in a building downtown and Stein was their leader, for a time. Guess he said that since he created them, he knew how to fight them. Food started running low, tempers high, and at some point they realized they weren't holed up but trapped."

"Stupid humans," Ros said, shaking his head. "Typical."

"Long story short, they decided Stein was the cause of their misery, so they took revenge. Can't say I blame them. They threw him over the fire escape, right into the stenches below."

Teeming masses. Quiet desperation.

"He didn't even hit the ground, there were so many of them. Of you, I mean. Gobbled him right up. Apparently, there was nothing left."

So Nietzsche was right: God is dead. And I had been looking forward to meeting my maker. He would have listened to me, understood my worth. I sat down in the driveway.

Ros must have seen the disappointment in my face. "We've still got each other, captain," he said. "We'll make it."

I stood up, gathering myself for the troops. They were counting on me to lead them.

I wrote: *Take us where we want to go. Or else!*

Pete squeezed his eyes shut. A tear traveled down his cheek.

I nudged his head with my toe. His eyes opened; I bit the air and moaned. I was a fierce and hungry zombie. A fiend. Hear me roar!

"Kill me," he said. "Just kill me already."

"No way, José," Ros said. "You drive."

Pete sighed. "Fine," he said. "Where to?"

Chicago, I wrote. I had to see it for myself.

CHAPTER SIXTEEN

BRAINS! BRAINS, I tell you. We needed a thalamus for the road. A frontal lobotomy. A side of cerebellum. A medulla oblongata. Anything to take our minds off the meat of Pete, who was lying supine on the street, curled in the cul-de-sac, a lamb for us wolves, as open and available as any whore.

Ros, Joan, and I waited for Annie and Guts to return. We did the zombie dance, circling around Pete like Native Americans in a peyote trance. I paused and wrote down my thoughts like a self-help housewife:

> This is my affirmation journal. My dream book. Captain's Log: Stardate: Zombie Apocalypse. Do not eat the human!

There was a gunshot followed by silence. Moans wafted through the subdivision like wind through an Aeolian harp.

Guts turned the corner onto Pawn Way. He was skipping, the feral's leg slung over one shoulder like a hobo's stick.

"Annie?" Ros asked, and Guts jerked his thumb in the direction he came from, imitating our gait and throwing in a few robotic dance moves and a moon walk. Show-off. He pulled a handful of brains out of his jeans pocket, which he proffered to me with his customary bow.

I smashed the red, hot sweetness into my face with both hands, smearing it on my cheeks. I could not get those brains into my mouth fast enough.

If I could breathe, I would have panted.

Ros and Joan went to town on the leg. From the garage, Eve resumed her moaning.

"Shut her up," Ros said.

Annie returned from the hunt, dragging the rest of the girl behind her by a rope; intestines hung around Annie's neck, bouncing against her budding breasts like Mardi Gras beads. Isaac stood, gripping the edge of his carriage, and shrieked. It was a loud and piercing sound.

"Stupid zombies," Ros said, a big toe hanging out the side of his mouth like a cigar stub. "Too loud."

Guts, our little caretaker, our golden boy, he gave Isaac the spleen. The baby sucked on it like a bottle.

"God help me," Pete said. "Here she comes."

I turned to see Eve shuffling toward Pete, her arms outstretched. The bandage had fallen off her stump of a wrist and it looked like a giant used tampon, black with blood. The senseless wench, the garden hose was still wrapped around her ankle. Her eyes were entirely yellow, as jaundiced as Marge Simpson. It was hard to believe I once loved her.

"Help!" Pete said, thrashing in an attempt to free himself.

"Only make it worse," Ros said.

Eve was almost upon him. Pete gagged when she growled. Oh, it was a close call. I contemplated shambling over there to restrain Eve, but, near as she was to her prey, I would never make it in time.

"Don't forget, Jack," Pete said. "You need me."

"Annie, get your gun," Ros said. Annie looked to me and I lifted a finger.

One bang and Eve's brains kaplooied all over Pete's face.

Muahahahaha, we all laughed. Like Count Chocula, it was a parody of villainous laughter, a simulacrum of evil mirth. Even Isaac was amused.

"Careful, Pete," Ros said. "That stuff's toxic."

"I am so fucked," Pete said, weeping into the concrete.

Welcome to the club, buddy.

PETE SAID GAS was getting scarce, but we had a full tank, plus a few cans we siphoned out of cars back in King's Court. We cruised east in a family van—the crew was in the back; I rode shotgun with Pete. There were so many obstacles in the road—body parts and zombies and cars—it was slow going.

None of us was wearing seatbelts. The glove compartment was stuffed with intestines and tendons and I had bite-sized bits of brain stored in my professor pockets. A McDonald's wrapper crunched under my feet; a copy of *The Zombie Survival Guide* was on the dash. In the back, Saint Joan stitched everyone up.

"She a doctor?" Pete asked.

No one answered.

I opened a book I'd found back in the subdivision, *'Salem's Lot*, Stephen King's vampire novel. As an academic, I had always thought King was beneath me. A typist, not a writer, to paraphrase Capote on Kerouac. I hadn't even felt it necessary to read him to form my opinion, though of course I'd seen the movies. I believed that anything with mass appeal was inherently bad, not only King, but Michael Jackson, Harry Potter, and the Dallas Cowboys cheerleaders. In my view, popularity proved inferiority, not worth.

But fifty million Elvis fans can't be wrong. The book was solid pop fiction, a page-turner, proving there was no such thing as a guilty pleasure anymore. I was eating people just like everyone else; that made us equal. I had become mainstream, a plebeian, the lowest common denominator, and I didn't care. In fact, it was liberating.

"Pete," Ros called from the backseat, tapping on the driver's headrest, "radio."

Pete turned the dial. Squawks. The honk of the Emergency Broadcast System. Another preacher. The Violent Femmes' "Blister in the Sun."

"Love this song," Ros said, bobbing his metal head.

"Who the hell is broadcasting this shit?" Pete asked.

"Why? What would you play?" Ros said.

"I'd give advice. Warnings. I'd try to help people. Tell 'em where to go. How to survive."

"Yeah," Ros gurgled, "get in a car with a bunch of zombies."

Pete looked in the rearview mirror. "It's a case of do as I say," he began.

Ros snarled and barked and Pete leaned forward as far as he could, his chest pressed against the steering wheel; Ros and Guts high-fived.

We rolled into the city and slowed to a crawl. Zombies surrounded us, rocking the vehicle, trying to plunder our human. The van inched forward.

"Punch it," Ros said. "Put the pedal to the metal."

I shook my head, pointing at Ros and then at the crowd. I turned my hand into a puppet and mimed talking, the thumb acting as the lower lip and the rest of the fingers yammering away. It was the signal Lucy used to give me whenever she was on the phone with her mother, a woman who lived to complain.

"No way," Ros said.

A zombie pressed her face against my window. She was chalk-white and covered with green and black bruises. She didn't look real; she looked like someone dressed up for Halloween.

I took out my pad and pen, wrote a quick note, and handed it to Pete.

"'Recruit them,'" Pete read. "'And ask about Stein.'"

"Bad idea," Ros said. "They'll get Pete."

"I agree," Pete said. "We should leave. Immediately."

I put my hands together in a pleading gesture. We couldn't see the street anymore, couldn't see Chicago's famed buildings or the sidewalks. All we could see were zombies, thicker than fog. But we had to try.

"'Need more soldiers,'" I wrote and Pete read out loud. "'That's an order.'"

"Yes, sir," Ros said, and slid open the van door. Arms groped inside like cilia.

"Annie?" Ros said, and Annie nailed a few in the head. Ros closed the door after him.

My window was stained with blood. I cracked it open but heard only the mob. Ros, if he was talking, was inaudible. Pete turned on the windshield wipers.

"I can't hear anything," he yelled, sticking his finger in his ear. "Those gunshots."

I turned around. Joan made a clucking sound, covered her ears, and indicated to Annie that she should holster her guns. Guts was kneeling on the seat vacated by Ros, his face and hands against the glass, trying to keep an eye on our soldier. I tugged on his shirt and he looked at me. I smiled, but he didn't smile back. He looked worried and angry, afraid that we'd lost Ros.

"I don't like this," Pete said. "Not one bit."

The door opened and Ros fell into the van. Guts scrambled out of his way as zombies spilled in like lemmings. Joan, Guts, Ros, and Annie fought them off, kicking them, Annie hitting their heads with the butt of her rifle.

"Drive!" Ros said. He pushed the last one out the door with his combat boot.

Pete took off. There were so many zombies we had no choice but to plow right through them. Their bodies thudded against the bumper, the van bouncing along as if on a lunar landscape.

"Too many," Ros said. "Crushed me."

Zombies could survive on the moon, I thought. We don't need oxygen or water. We could be happy there, lying on our backs in a crater, watching the earth spin in its lazy circle. Or better still, we could escape gravity and float through space for eternity, witnessing the births and deaths of galaxies and stars. Waltzing to the pulse of red dwarfs and quarks. Joining the tail of a comet and traveling to the beginning of time, we could meet God there.

Eat God there too.

"They didn't understand," Ros said. "Stupid zombies."

I missed Lucy. And I missed being human. We were part of something larger now, something as timeless and inevitable as death. Or as death used to be. We had already changed the world.

CHAPTER SEVENTEEN

WE DROVE NORTH on 41, following the shoreline, running away. It was Plan B, but I had to separate us from the throng in Chicago. I needed solitude to think.

Out the window was Lake Michigan, big as the ocean. The sky was battleship gray and cloudless, and the water was choppy, with whitecaps surfacing here and there like fierce fish. There weren't any birds.

For miles and miles, there was nothing but zombies. At night, the thinner ones froze. During the day, what with the sun and global warming, they thawed and wandered around.

Our future as northerners was predictable: freeze in the winter; reanimate in the spring. Like tulips.

There's resurrection in April, T. S. Eliot's cruelest month, breeding lilacs and zombies out of the dead land.

But I worried about the long wasteland of winter. When frozen, would we be comatose or conscious? A patient etherized upon a table or a woman trapped in a man's body, too poor for hormone therapy, making do with false eyelashes and size 13 heels? If we were locked in a vessel we couldn't control, it would be torture.

It was safe and warm in the vehicle; with the heat blasting and the sun beaming, we had our own greenhouse effect.

When we stopped for gas, we had to protect Pete. Annie shot the ghouls, our brothers, encroaching slow as starfish, and every shot was dead-on, every time.

Forgive me for shooting the zombies; they were so stupid and so cold.

There were no humans or military convoys in sight. No authorities for us to confront. Outside of the car, it was anarchy. Survival of the fittest.

Next to me, Pete was eating Donut Gems, the white powder clinging to his beard, the crinkle of the plastic wrap insanely loud in the quiet of the car. I could hear his jaw pop and crack as he chewed; I listened to him swallow. In my lap, Stephen King's vampires continued to suck blood.

Do not eat the human . . . do not eat the human . . . do not eat. . .

Suddenly a squeal followed by a low moan from the backseat. The mating call of a beluga whale. Guts lunged for Pete, wrapping his skinny arm around both the driver's headrest and Pete's neck. The car careened toward the median.

"Get him off me!" Pete yelled.

Saint Joan grabbed Guts by the shirttails and pulled him to her. Guts moaned and whimpered, the cry of a baby left on a doorstep, while Joan cuddled him, rubbing his back. Small comfort. Guts rested his head on her breasts, folding himself into her, his shoulders heaving as if he were sobbing.

"Kid has a point," Ros said. "Hungry."

"Fuck you," Pete said. "Get back to your drooling."

I held my hand up, indicating peace, truce, love, we're in this together, gang.

Truth was, though, Pete was looking mighty tasty. Every time I glanced his way, he turned into a cartoon steak or pork chop.

Don't hate the player; hate the game.

"The stench in here," Pete said, rolling down his window. "God! You guys stink."

Ros put his thumbs in his ears and wiggled his fingers at the back of Pete's delicious head. Pete took off his green cap and scratched at his scalp. Dead skin flew. I stuck out my tongue, hoping to catch some like snowflakes.

"I'm tired," Pete said. "I need to sleep. Someplace safe." He replaced his cap. "And alone," he added.

I nodded. I longed to touch his shoulder in reassurance but I didn't dare. Touching leads to grabbing and grabbing leads to biting and biting leads to eating and before you know it, your driver is gone.

Pete exited at the next service area and pulled into a Comfort Inn. He found the keys and the room.

We were in Wisconsin, near Manitowoc. Land of cheese.

"Can she stand guard?" Pete asked, pointing at Annie.

We looked at her. She touched the gun at her hip.

"Just a few hours," Pete said.

"Sweet dreams!" Ros said.

Pete slammed the bolt into place and moved furniture in front of the door.

"What?" Ros called. "Don't you trust us?"

The parking lot was full of abandoned cars and melting snow. The frontage road was deserted. The humans had either been eaten to the marrow or fled. And no humans meant no zombies.

"What's the plan, captain?"

The plan?

Here's a plan for you: After the bomb drops, live securely in your shelter with enough canned food for a century—but, oops, no can opener! Or be the last man on earth, finally alone with your precious books—and, oops, break your glasses!

This world was an episode of *The Twilight Zone*.

The plan, my dear Ros, was simple: Walk around in circles, drooling and moaning, until we stumble upon some hapless human to devour.

Or decay until we're nothing but walking, chattering bones.

Or shoot each other in the brains and end our misery.

The real plan, the ultimate plan, was to wake from this eternal nightmare, cozy in bed with Lucy beside me, and drink a hot cup of coffee while reading the morning paper. After a breakfast of eggs and toast, the plan was to walk to the university and deliver a ninety-minute lecture deconstructing Britney Spears's new haircut.

Ros, Joan, and I shuffled into the lobby. Ros turned on the radio. "Chin up," he said. "Soldier on."

Guts was playing with Isaac in the circular drive outside, tossing the baby up high and catching him. I considered stopping them—what if Guts missed?—but Isaac's mouth was open as if laughing and besides, we were invincible. Almost.

If ever there was a time for an old-fashioned wooden deus ex machina. . .

I waited for it to descend from the sky. I looked out the window. Guts threw Isaac up in the air and wandered off, distracted by something. The baby splatted on the ground, rolling like a burrito. A grub worm. Olive Oyl's Sweet Pea all bundled in his blue blanket.

Ros fiddled with the dial. Nothing. No ghost in that machine. No savior.

We had to save ourselves.

"And then I carried my son upstairs," a woman's voice said, bursting out of the radio, "and locked him in his room."

"How old is he?" asked another woman.

"Ten."

"Where is he now?"

"He's still in there. He's moaning, banging on the door."

"Here's what you do, here's what you have to do."

The mother sobbed. "I know what I have to do! The problem is I can't do it."

"Gwen," the woman said, "calm down and listen to me . . ."

"What if they discover a cure? What if he's alive in there somewhere? He's my baby. My only son."

Ros rolled his eyes. "Cry me a river," he said.

But Joan put her hands over her bosom. The old broad was touched.

"You're a survivor, Gwen," the woman on the radio said. "You've made it this far. You are strong. You can do this!"

"Kids?" Ros asked Joan.

Joan held up three fingers.

"One of each," Ros said.

So I'd been wrong about Joan and her spinsterhood, as I'd been wrong about everything so far: Eve. Stein. Our future. Even Stephen King. What other lies had I told myself? What lies do I continue to believe?

"Is there a man about the house?" the woman asked Gwen.

"Not anymore," Gwen said. "Shit, shooting that bastard was easy. Right between the eyes."

The women laughed. Ros switched off the radio.

"Things have changed," he said.

He was right. If there was talk radio. . .

"Miss my girlfriend," he said.

And I didn't even know Ros's real name.

"We met in high school," he gurgled. "Drama club. We were doing *Grease*—Becky played Frenchie. I built sets, moved stuff around. Grunt work. What I'm good at."

Frenchie. The Beauty School Dropout. I gestured for Ros to go on.

"Becky wasn't the most beautiful girl in town," he continued. "But she was mine and I loved her."

Ros wheezed and pressed his diaphragm. It was the most I'd heard him say at once and it appeared to give him pain.

"Ooorrmmph," said Joan.

"Wonder where she is now." Ros rested his chin in his hand. His fingers disappeared into his cheek. "Dead or undead." His skin was raw, splotched with lesions and pus. "You made me this way," he said, looking at me.

I shrugged my shoulders. Guilty as charged.

Ros walked over. He opened his arms and embraced me. "I'm glad," he said. "Brothers. You and me."

I extended an arm to Joan and she joined us.

"Group hug," Ros said, resting his metal head on my fortified shoulder. "Feels good."

IN THE LOBBY, we gave up. We sat around and slobbered, our eyes vacant and weeping yellow. Until we heard a gunshot outside. Then another and another.

"Annie," Ros said.

It took minutes to get off the couch. Long minutes to walk to the door. More minutes to open it. Isaac was still stuck on the circular drive. We left him there, a caterpillar in his cocoon.

There was a cluster of undead advancing on Annie, zeroing in on Pete's room. Annie was holding them off, blowing their brains out, but the moans and shots would attract more. Behind the door, I could hear Pete moving furniture.

"Stay in there," Ros yelled. "Not safe."

Pete opened the door anyway, armed with the metal towel rack from the bathroom, some straightened wire hangers, and a chair. Clever man looked like a lion tamer.

There were five zombies left, not counting us. Pete raced to the closest, and—wham!—whacked her upside the head with the towel rack. The fixture broke in half—cheap motel shit—and the zombette kept coming. Pete jammed the clothes hanger in her eye, pushing it in and twisting. The eye popped out and she fell.

"Aww," Ros said. "She looked like a nice girl."

Annie took care of the remaining undead lickety-split. Bam! Bam! Bam! Bam!

Surely she was running out of bullets.

Screaming like a television Indian chief, sneaky Pete lunged for Annie and plunged the coat hanger into her neck, thrusting it up under her helmet and into her head. But he must've missed her brain stem, because nothing happened.

Annie rammed the gun into Pete's stomach. The trigger clicked. Empty.

Out of somewhere, out of nowhere, out of the very ether, Guts raced up, hunched low like a football player, and bit Pete in the ankle.

How I loved that ankle biter, the crumb crusher. Our adorable imp.

Pete collapsed. There was no turning back now. We pounced on our driver, peeling him open like an orange. He screamed like no orange I've ever heard.

It was a Sunday family dinner: Joan gripping Pete's glistening something or other in her hands like a raccoon, blood dripping down her chin; Guts pulling out yards and yards of guts, rolling around in them, biting them; Ros holding Pete's lungs aloft like Lady Justice; and Annie, sweet young thing, Annie had captured his heart, which looked fake, like an anatomical gummi heart— gelatinous, chewy, and chock-full of high-fructose corn syrup.

As for me, the patriarch, I sat at the head of the table. Pete's hair stuck to the roof of my mouth and in between my teeth like corn silk. I cracked his skull like a pecan. Sweet nut of the brain underneath. Baby Isaac wailed from the circular drive in front of the motel, but we all ignored him. It was a zombie-eat-human world; charity was for the weak. And any second, another wave of the undead might show up and take our booty.

We ate all of Pete. He deserved it, the Judas. Betrayer. We took our time, savoring him like a seven-course meal. The sun went down and came up at least once, but we barely noticed. Pete's blood kept us from freezing. Annie paused occasionally to reload and pick off approaching zombies. At some point, Guts retrieved Isaac and set him next to the body so the baby could take suck. Isaac whined and nestled against Pete's chest.

Afterward we lay around Pete's hair, bones, teeth, and ball cap, his skeleton picked clean, a Thanksgiving turkey carcass. Hardly enough left for soup.

"Could use floss," Ros said.

The sun was setting. I wanted to get up and move to the hotel, but Pete's meat weighed me down. I rolled onto my back; the sky was purple; Venus was visible. The stars were popping out like fireflies. A plane whooshed by, flying low.

A plane?

"Captain," Ros said, "that's a bomber."

There was a human struggle in this war. I often forgot them. The other side. Enemy mine. How many of them were fighting for their lives that very minute? Scavenging for food and protecting their Isaacs. How many of them were looking up at those same stars—in Illinois, New York, Mexico, Iraq?

It began to snow. It began to sleet. In the distance, an explosion. The stars disappeared.

"They're bombing Milwaukee," Ros said.

The humans' retreat was over. War was back on.

CHAPTER EIGHTEEN

THEY BOMBED ALL night: firebombs, cluster bombs, smart bombs, cherry bombs, bang and boom, shock and awe. We loafed in the parking lot at our ease, observing the display. It was the Fourth of July and New Year's Eve rolled into one. It was a song of destruction. The heat from the blasts kept us from turning into slushies.

"Any undead in there are toast," Ros said.

It was just as well. What would they have done? Build cities? Design furniture? Form governments? Make pottery?

Zombies are not creators. Zombies don't manipulate and control the environment. We don't organize day laborers or deplete the ozone layer. We don't build dams or run for city council. We don't play softball or pinball. We are Zen masters. Like a Venus flytrap, just give us meat and more meat.

Feed me, Seymour!

"Barely remember being human anymore," Ros said. "I remember stuff that happened, but like in a movie."

Joan patted his shoulder. Her face was melted wax, her breasts pale shadows of their former stand-at-attention glory. She had fed three children with those dugs and they were rotting now, the worst kind of cancer.

"I was in Baghdad," Ros continued, "and one day, they were like, you're going home, soldier. Bigger fish to fry in the States. I was glad to get out of the desert. Felt lucky to be alive and going home to Becky."

Annie rolled onto her stomach. Her pigtails were stained red and stiff with blood and guts. She looked like a girl the Ramones might have sung about.

"But home was way worse than al-Qaeda," Ros said. "Everyone dead or undead."

Used to be you were either alive or dead. Pregnant or not pregnant. Not anymore. Now everybody's liminal. Everyone's a transsexual.

Annie made an hourglass figure with her hands and pointed to Ros. "Burrawwheee?" she asked.

"Never found her," he said.

The bombing stopped, the ground rumbled. In the distance, an engine roared.

"Tank," Ros said.

"Come and get us, scum suckers!" a voice yelled.

My bite site tingled. The army was advancing, clanging a bell, making a racket. Their plan was obvious: Flush us out and shoot us.

I pantomimed a vague plan of escape, anchored around this basic premise: Must Get Away Now! Guts gathered up Isaac and zoomed ahead. The rest of us picked our sorry selves off the ground and followed.

Joan, Ros, Annie, and I plodded along, bringing pestilence, war, famine, and death—but at a glacial pace, the velocity of slugs. Call us the Four Retarded Horsemen of the Apocalypse. It might take us a while, but eventually we'll kill and eat you. Relax while you wait— have a cannoli.

Zombies emerged from houses and basements, from underneath piles of wood and rubble. Lured by the promise of human flesh, they headed straight into the military's trap. We passed them on the street and I tried to look as many as possible in the eye, searching for a glimmer of light, anything brighter than the dirty yellow film that blinded them.

There was nothing. No one home. They were deader than dead. At least they would keep the army occupied while we escaped. To where or what was another question.

WE CONTINUED NORTH, away from the tanks. It was still snowing. Annie slipped and fell on the ice and it took all of us to get her up. Guts stayed a few blocks ahead, scouting locations, searching for humans, military or civilian, to either chomp on or avoid.

We were in a state of nature now: kill or be killed.

We passed a frozen zombie on the side of the road. Joan paused to examine it—the gender was indeterminate, the creature decayed to not much more than patches of skin and tendons clinging to a skeleton.

More planes flew overhead. Leaflets dropped from one of them. ATTENTION, it read. THE OUTBREAK IS UNDER CONTROL. THE VIRUS IS CONTAINED. THE ENEMY IS BEING ISOLATED AND ELIMINATED. FOR YOUR OWN PROTECTION, STAY AWAY FROM URBAN AREAS. THE U.S. GOVERNMENT HAS SET UP BASES IN MOST STATES. TURN ON YOUR RADIO TO FIND THE ONE NEAREST YOU AND MAKE YOUR WAY THERE IMMEDIATELY. STAY IN OPEN AREAS AND BE ALERT AT ALL TIMES!

At the bottom was a graphic of a stick-figure human running from a gang of zombies. The caption read: DO NOT APPROACH THE ENEMY. IF YOU CAN AVOID A CONFRONTATION BY RUNNING AWAY, THEN RUN AWAY. IF YOU ARE CORNERED, DESTROY THE ENEMY'S BRAIN BY SHOOTING, STABBING, BLUDGEONING, OR BURNING.

"What's it say?" Ros asked.

I shook my head. It was too complicated and depressing to explain that we were a virus.

"We're losing," Ros said.

I nodded. We shuffled on, but it was becoming harder and harder to move. The wind felt like a wall and there was an inch of snow piled on my shoulder. We caught up to Guts and he handed me Isaac. The baby was frozen solid. An ice puck. I tossed him to Joan, who put him in her doctor's bag.

"Wait," Ros said. We stopped. Annie swayed like a pine in the harsh winter wind. If we stayed still much longer, we'd freeze in the middle of the highway, and it was dawning on me that freezing was not our best option. At least not out in the open, where the army would eventually find us and blow our brains out.

The best laid plans of zombies and men. . .

Ros pointed east. "The lake," he said. "Jump in the lake."

It was a good idea. Winter at the bottom of the lake, then walk into the sunshine come spring. Primordial creatures crawling out of the slime.

We turned right and headed for Lake Michigan. We were survivors, refugees, and just desperate enough to take the Polar Bear Plunge.

DOWNTOWN MANITOWOC WAS lovely. It's on the lake, with a courthouse and a park with swings and a gazebo, plus a museum and marinas. It was white with snow, pure as a sno-globe winter scene. Stores lined the street: Urban Outfitters, Starbucks, the Gap, Williams-Sonoma, all of them with their windows broken and doors wide open. Money strewn on the floors. The credit card machines and cash registers silenced.

Joan ushered us into an REI and Ros, our soldier, helped all of us select waterproof jackets, pants, and caps—anything to slow down the rate of decay. We could be underwater for months.

Guts took off his jeans and T-shirt. His little body was ravaged. Lesions all over like an AIDS patient. Bruised pieces of flesh like old fruit. The duct tape holding in his guts was coming undone; bullet holes dotted his back like stigmata.

"Do I look like that?" Ros asked.

Underneath our clothes, we all looked like that; underneath the patches Joan had sewn over our bullet holes, under my Jason-mask shoulder and Ros's metal head and Joan's suede knee and Annie's patched ass, we were rotting corpses. We could never forget it.

Joan opened her doctor's bag. Isaac's head popped out like a whack-a-mole. Thawed, immaculate, and as complete as the day he was born, he wouldn't need any repairs.

"Help us, Joan," Ros said, holding out his hands in supplication. The Virgin Mary lawn statuary pose. Joan threaded her needle.

She worked on Annie first and when the teenager was as good as new, I stationed her at the door. The army wasn't too far behind us and we needed a guard. A few zombies tottered down the sidewalk, bunched together in groups of two or three. I made sure Annie understood she should look out for humans and alert me if any approached. She brought her hand to her forehead in a salute.

I helped Joan with Guts, holding his intestines in place while she stitched his stomach. I considered removing his innards entirely. We could store them in a canopic jar, mummifying them for future archaeologists.

Why not remove all of our vital organs, leaving only brains and bones? Intestines, liver, lungs, stomach, we didn't need them. Isn't that how King Tut remained so gloriously intact for centuries? Wouldn't that preserve us?

I walked like an Egyptian, trying to communicate my idea to Ros and Joan. In the distance, there were gunshots.

"No time for dancing," Ros said. "Army's coming."

I looked over to Annie to see if she could give us a status update. She wasn't there. I shook Ros's elbow and pointed to where the teenage zombie had been.

"Annie?" he asked. I shrugged my shoulders and shambled to the door. Outside, there was only the blue of the lake and a smattering of aimless corpses, wandering around like the people you see on television whose homes have been destroyed by tornadoes or hurricanes, standing in what used to be their living rooms, looking for birth certificates or wedding photos, any remains of their past lives.

Ros was right behind me. "Annie!" he said as loudly as he could. He sounded like a goat.

"Where is she?" he asked. I shook my head. "We have to look for her." I nodded my assent.

Joan and Guts joined us at the door. "Kid," Ros said to Guts, "you run. Cover ground. Captain, you go north, I'll go south. Nurse, stay here with the baby. Annie may come back."

I shook my head.

"It's a good plan," Ros gurgled.

I shook my head again, adding my arm and finger to the gesture. Because splitting up would be a mistake. It happens in every disaster movie or thriller, every horror and slasher flick. The core group members go in separate directions to find the missing person or search for an exit or locate the cell phone or radio or a weapon. The killer takes advantage of their solitude, picking each character off at his leisure, going for the weakest ones first.

Divide and conquer. I wouldn't let it happen to us.

I put my arms around Ros, Joan, and Guts and held them close. Ros tried to squirm away, but I would not let go. We had to stick together.

"You're the boss," Ros said.

We walked out of the store and headed north. Isaac was in a carrier on Joan's back. Joan put her arm around my waist and gave me a squeeze; I held Ros firmly by his jacket, afraid he would try to escape from my grasp.

There were more gunshots, each round louder than the one before.

"Stupid," Ros said. "They'll get all of us this way."

We stumbled forward.

"Kid," Ros said, shaking Guts's shoulder. "Run! Find Annie!"

Before I could stop him, Guts was off, racing down the main street, jogging past the high-end stores like a star athlete, putting distance between us and him.

"Our only chance," Ros said. "Sorry."

Guts turned a corner and disappeared. I looked behind us. We'd gone a paltry fifty feet.

"He'll find her," Ros said. "She's slow."

Ros was right. Annie couldn't have gone far. We crawled back to the REI and waited.

THE AIR BEGAN to hum and buzz, as if someone had flipped a switch and turned on the electricity. Our bite sites tingled. The army couldn't be too far off. In the street, zombies began walking in the same direction, with determination and purpose, heading straight for the humans. Like rats leaving a sinking ship, they were going to meet their second death halfway.

Not us, though. We stayed hidden in the REI, oozing slime on the trendy camping chairs, trying to ignore the call of the wild.

Ros wandered around the store, adding flippers and a snorkeling mask to his underwater gear.

"Help me breathe," he joked as he snapped the mask on.

Joan shuffled over to the window and I heaved myself out of my chair. If we waited much longer, we'd either give in and join the herd or be discovered by a reconnaissance unit. Neither option was acceptable. I made a swimming motion with my arms.

"Roger that," Ros said.

We opened the door. Down the road we could see the zombies of Wisconsin heading south, a giant flock of stinking flightless birds.

"Bye-bye," Ros said, waving at their backs. "Good luck."

He pressed on his diaphragm and opened his mouth to give it one last try. "Annie!" he bellowed.

Joan poked his stomach with her elbow, cutting his cry short. She pointed down the street.

The children were walking toward us, Guts skipping and jumping. They waved, big smiles on their adorable faces, greeting us like dead grandparents welcoming their descendants to heaven. Annie twirled in a circle like a music-box ballerina.

Wherever she'd been, I didn't care. Even though she disobeyed me, I was elated to see her. She was forgiven.

ROS, JOAN, AND I dragged our raggedy asses across the park. Isaac was encased in the waterproof pack on Joan's back. So snugly wrapped, he was invisible.

It started raining and it must have been cold. Our feet squeaked on the sand.

"You," Ros said, shaking his fist at Annie when we met them at the lake.

Annie went through a series of pantomimes describing her adventure. From what I could gather, she'd picked up the scent of a human and took off after him, thinking that a meal was in order before our watery sojourn. She'd found him in the Crate and Barrel, but as she drew near, he crossed the line from human to zombie. She wrinkled her nose to express her distaste.

While she acted out the scene, I tied all of us together with nylon rope. I didn't want to lose anyone again.

"Scared us half to death," Ros said. "Bad girl!"

I tried to look severe, but I couldn't. I felt warm and fuzzy inside and I hugged Annie close, pressing her head against my breast.

We heard a barrage of machine-gun fire. There was no more time for sentiment.

Thin sheets of ice floated on top of the lake and a few chunks washed up on shore. Annie bent down, picked up a handful of sand, and let it sift through her fingers. Guts skipped a rock, but the water was too choppy to count the number of times it skimmed the surface. Joan had her eyes fixed on the horizon.

"Baaaahhhhhee," she said, pointing. I squinted in the direction of her finger but couldn't see anything.

"Is that a boat?" Ros asked. "Or ship?"

I could see only gray: gray sky, gray lake, gray clouds like great gray brains.

"Destroyer," Ros said. "I think."

Annie brandished one of her guns. She aimed and shot; the bullet fell far short.

"It's way far away," Ros said, "but good eye."

My heart sank like a battleship. Not much had gone right for us. If current trends continued, we'd be shot when we rose from the lake in the spring. Hunted and gunned down like animals.

And I didn't want to die again. I wanted to emerge from the water a great leader, a visionary capable of bringing my people out of the wilderness and into the Promised Land.

This was my dream, my grand solution: Negotiate with the humans. Find our common ground and reach an uneasy peace, explaining that we, too, are God's children. And as such, we have a right to exist. Since we need brains, offer to eat their criminals, their invalids, their suicides and car crash victims. Stillborns, abortions, vegetables. Anyone expendable. We'd be performing a valuable service, when you thought about it. And when the zombie population dwindled as a result of decay or insurgent attacks, we'd bite a few humans and allow them to join our ranks. My guess was there would be no dearth of volunteers. In fact, over time, being selected would become an honor or ritual, a part of their culture, like in Shirley Jackson's "The Lottery."

We could live forever that way. Symbiotically. It wasn't perfect—no compromise is—but it was a start.

Guts began walking into the lake. When the water reached his ankles, he looked over his shoulder and held out his hands. I stepped forward, hoping to walk on water. No such luck. I grabbed one of Guts's hands; Joan took the other. Annie and Ros joined us and we formed a chain. We could have been a group of actors pretending to be a normal American family on vacation, ready to take a winter swim together at some fabulous lakeside resort. Or we could have actually been that family, no more simulations or acting, no layers of meaning and artifice sprinkled with postmodern allusions. The birth of the real.

A zombie is a zombie is a zombie is a zombie.

Full-immersion baptism. We shambled into the water like characters in a Flannery O'Connor short story. I glanced at Joan. She didn't look like herself in her forest-green water gear. Without her nurse's uniform, she could have been any zombie; her noble nose was mostly gone, her skin a crazy quilt of brown blood. But her medical bag was snug in a waterproof backpack, alongside Isaac.

We kept walking. The water reached Guts's waist, his chest, his brave little chin. I didn't feel wet, although I was halfway in; I didn't feel anything.

"Hold your breath, little man," Ros said as Guts went under.

Soon enough we were all underwater where it was dark and murky. There must have been fish but I didn't see any. Not at first. Ros said something, and the sound came in waves, washing over me like sonar, like dolphins talking. I wanted to give him the thumbs-up but didn't dare let go of Annie and Guts. They were my lifeline. My future. My underwater breathing apparatus.

We were in limbo, wandering the bottom of Lake Michigan. A lost tribe of sodden zombies, we were prehistoric. Dinosaurs. I tried to steer us north, but I've never had a good sense of direction.

My eyes adjusted to the dark. A school of shiny yellow fish surrounded us. One ventured forward and nibbled on Guts's neck. Then another. I shooed them away.

Here was a contingency I hadn't thought of: What if we were eaten by fish?

The belly of the whale, that I could handle. Being devoured by a leviathan is biblical and grand, full of history and tradition. Think *Moby Dick,* Jonah, *Jaws, Orca, Lake Placid* and *Lake Placid 2.* Even Godzilla lived in the sea.

But being nibbled on by a school of small fry was beneath me. As a mythical being, I would not accept a demise less than epic. I jerked us away from the school.

And the lake turned deeper and a shade darker. The current was as strong as the ocean. There was a rip tide or an undertow, and I was lifted up by it. I let go of my comrades' hands.

We let the water take us. It was effortless, this dance. I wiggled my body like an eel. Annie and Guts were doing the same—Joan and Ros were too far away to see, but I could feel their weight tugging on the rope around my waist. The five of us were one creature, each part of a greater whole, fingers on a hand, tentacles of a giant squid, cogs in a machine.

It was like flying. Jonathon Livingdead Seagull. There was freedom underwater. We went where the lake sent us.

A speckled fish passed between Guts and me; it had a pink stripe down its side like a Nike swoosh. Then a salmon, steel gray and bigger than Isaac, its mouth shaped like a bottle opener. He gave us the fish-eye and moved on.

We could swim forever this way, I thought. To the ends of the earth. To the ocean or the gulf. Until the water gets shallow and the weather turns warm and we crawl onto the shore, a little worse for the wear, but still striving, still bleating our clarion cry for brains and more brains. For life.

CHAPTER NINETEEN

WE FLOATED AND swam like mermaids. I slipped in and out of consciousness, half-frozen and half-Buddha, one step closer to nirvana and pure being.

I was a butterfly, a jellyfish. My life as a human grew more and more remote. The trappings of culture, all we created, the whole bloated project of humanity, from the pyramids to Frank Gehry, Pindar to Bukowski, suet to sushi, all of it as ephemeral as an Etch-A-Sketch. Like Ros, I remembered random events from my past as if they had happened to someone in a movie.

As children, my sister and I spent a few weeks every summer with Oma and Opa in their cottage in Seattle. It smelled like lavender potpourri and boiled meat. The four of us played Scrabble and Oma always won, clasping her thick fingers together and bringing them to her lips as she studied the board.

"We escaped the camps," she said, "so you could be here, *kleine* Jack. Safe and happy with us."

When Oma and Opa died, they left my father a sizable legacy of property, stocks and bonds, old money from Austria, plus new money they'd earned in America. When my father and mother died, that legacy was passed down to my sister and me. Although I'd produced no heirs of my own, my sister had two sons set to inherit our world.

Or did she? And whose world was it? My nephews and my sister, were they alive, dead, or living dead? Animal, vegetable, or mineral?

We passed over a wondrous fish feeding on the bottom. It must have been seven feet long, coral pink, with spikes on its back like a dragon. It didn't look up at us, just continued to suck on the sand like an aquatic vacuum cleaner. No doubt that species of fish has lived unchanged for millennia, eating whatever settles on lake bottoms, and growing and maturing as a result. Releasing eggs in the spring, reproducing, then getting old and dying. Perfect in its design, no need to evolve. Like a cockroach or an alligator.

I rolled my torso, undulating. I could feel Ros pulling on us, his flippers an advantage in this environment. I pulled on the rope, bringing Guts closer to me. A snail was on his cheek and I ripped it off.

Zombies are the next step in human evolution. The virus, our birth, the apocalyptic mad scientist shtick—no Frankenstein's creature or end of the world, but a giant leap forward. Progress. Like Vonnegut's *Galápagos*, back to the sea.

We eat but don't grow. We reproduce but don't need eggs or mitosis, ejaculation or even love. We are as simple as fish. Simpler than fish.

And as Henry Zombie Thoreau said: simplify, simplify, simplify.

We swam past another fish, this one about half the size of Guts. It was the color of a tin can with a splash of orange on its fins. I reached out and grabbed it under the gills. The fish thrashed; its tail was strong and slapped my shoulder, but I brought it to me.

The first bite yielded a mouthful of scales. The second bite was all bone, but I ripped through it anyway. Because the third bite hit braindirt: minuscule, grainy, and cold. Entirely unsatisfying. Like jerking off instead of screwing; playing checkers instead of chess; watching Gus Van Sant's shot-by-shot remake of *Psycho*. Looking at a photograph of *Guernica*.

Still, I ate the fish. You take what you can get. The water turned pink with its blood and the gang gathered round, hungry for stink.

We chewed on its stomach, intestines, tail, fins, spine, the solid meat of its sides. What I wouldn't have given for hot brains. Ros popped a fish eye in his mouth and said something that sounded like, "Needs wasabi."

That's why I loved Ros. Like his namesake, he was comic relief.

A FLASHBACK, PRE-ZOMBIE. As vivid as reality. Lucid dreaming. Lucy dreaming.

"Jack?" Lucy asked, her voice lilting up at the end of my name. "Why did you marry me?"

I closed the book I'd been reading, marking my place with my thumb: Rene Descartes's *Principles of Philosophy*.

"Can someone say high-maintenance?" I said, laughing. "You know why."

We were in my study with its book-lined walls, big oak desk, Persian rug, Macintosh laptop, and antique china hutch loaded with pop culture ephemera—my Pez collection, a Sigmund Freud action figure, a can of Billy Beer, a Magic 8 Ball. Lucy was dusting, although she didn't have to. Someone came in once a week.

"We can't reproduce," she said. "Isn't that what marriage is for? To start a family?"

"Tell that to our gay friends."

"Touché."

Lucy had just suffered her third miscarriage, and the doctors warned it would likely happen again.

"I married you," I said, "so no one else could have you. It was a selfish endeavor."

Lucy wiped my vintage Archies lunch box with an old sock. "Have you thought more about adopting?" she asked.

I put the book on my desk and gave her my full attention. Her dark hair stuck up in the back like Alfalfa's. She was trying not to cry.

"C'mere," I said, and held out my arms. She snuggled onto my lap and buried her face in my neck. Her bony ass jutted into my thigh. She was all bones and heart, that girl. Bones and heart.

"I don't want some stranger's baby," she whispered. "I want my own."

I rubbed her back and petted her short hair. It had been a tough week, a tough year. For Lucy especially.

"Do you want to keep trying?" I asked. "I'm game if you are."

"I'll probably fail again."

"Don't say that. You didn't fail," I said. "How about concentrating on your writing? You could finish your novel."

"My novel is nothing but self-involved drivel. It's not gonna change the world."

"In all honesty, neither is a child."

"But ours would be special. It would grow up to cure cancer. Or AIDS."

"Or start a major war."

"We could raise a Hitler!"

"Or a radio talk show host," I said.

"Maybe I'm not meant to be a mom."

"Nobody's meant to be anything. And even if we had a kid, what then? He would be born, grow up, be happy sometimes, sad mostly, become bitter as he aged and didn't realize his dreams, and then die old and alone. That's it. End of story."

"Don't forget take up space and use valuable resources."

"You're absolutely right. Every human being is a drain on the ecosystem. We're overrunning the planet as it is. Perhaps it's for the best."

Lucy refused to give up, however. We tried for the next several months, but I ate her before she could get pregnant again. For that I'm glad: Her barren womb nurtured me when I needed it most.

CHAPTER TWENTY

DAYS PASSED, WEEKS, a month, who knows? Water is timeless and we were part of it, adrift in the soup of it, barely aware, eating fish only when the hunger became unbearable.

Way above us, there was the shadow of a boat. Ros pulled me to him and pointed to it. The five of us gathered together and kicked upward. We were frogmen, navy SEALs, Ros's flippers doing most of the hard work. As we neared the surface, sun. Light sparkling on the lake. A sky-blue sky with wisps of high clouds.

I poked my forehead and eyes out of the water. The others did the same, staying mostly submerged, like computer-generated soldiers in a video game. One of Joan's eyeballs was filmed over with weeds like a grass eye-patch. Ros's metal head was warped and rusty.

We swam up to the vessel, which was a sailboat, a yacht actually, thirty or forty feet long. I poked my whole head out of the lake. *Maria Sangria* read the script painted on the side.

It was quiet out of the water, without the pressure of the lake. A breeze whistled in my ear. No sounds came from the boat and I didn't sense any humans on it either; my shoulder was calm, dead flesh. As tingly as a T-bone. There was no shore that I could see.

Water water everywhere; we were right in the middle of the lake.

Ros pulled us around *Maria Sangria* until we found the anchor. Annie kept slipping underwater; we all did. Zombies aren't good swimmers. We sink like tombstones.

I pointed at Guts, then at the rope attached to the anchor. Joan and I set Guts free, untying his metaphorical umbilical cord, and the urchin shimmied on up.

"Look at him go," Ros said, his voice deep and wet as a sea monster's.

We did our best to keep each other afloat, but Ros kept drifting away. Joan held out her hand and he grabbed it. We pulled him back into our bobbing circle.

Treading water with my friends, I lifted my face up to the heavens, letting the sun dry my skin, which was flapping from being so long submerged. I felt an optimism I'd never experienced as a human. My soul was clear and sweet. We were elemental creatures—water, wind, earth, fire.

Professor Jack would've made an Earth, Wind and Fire joke here, inserting a song title or an ironic comment on their costumes or cultural significance. Zombie Jack refrains.

"Mooooooo!" Guts lowed from *Maria Sangria*, throwing a rope ladder over the side. We made our way over to it and hauled ourselves up, but it was hard going, particularly for Annie. Ros helped her, his hand cupping her half ass, pushing her up while caressing the bite site on her ankle. Those days underwater had diminished her cognition and they certainly hadn't helped her coordination.

This is your brain, the Reagan-era public service announcement goes. This is your brain as a waterlogged zombie.

Like a pirate, I landed on deck and searched the boat. Avast! And ahoy! Food! Old, desiccated, wrinkly, salty, tough food. Starved to death, perhaps. Or dehydrated. But who cared? One in a deck chair; another facedown on the ground. Two more reclining on cots in the cabin. A male in a yellow slicker, probably the captain, slumped over the wheel.

Human jerky. One for each of us.

"Bon appétit!" said Ros.

I went for the woman in the chair. She was middle-aged and had once been fat, judging from the excess skin. I stood behind her, my legs wobbly and sliding around on the wet deck. I put my hands over her ears, pulled up with all my strength, and screwed off her head.

You've seen this scene in a million movies: the unnatural red of the human's veins and tendons glisten and throb as the head is liberated from the body; the victim screams before, during, and even after the procedure. The proverbial chicken. Quite often the beheading is presented as comeuppance or karma for premarital sex or mistreating women or abusing power. In other words, the victim is a bad, immoral human who deserves death by zombies, death by Leatherface, death by vampires or giant spiders.

There was no narrative significance to this decapitation, however. The lady had been long dead: No blood flowed from her grisly neck; no justice was served. I neither knew nor cared whether she was kind to children and small animals, whether she was faithful to her husband or spent too much money on her clothing. Whether she survived as long as she had at the expense of others or because she saved others.

All I knew was her brains tasted like chocolate cheesecake does to a dieter. A little slice of heaven.

"Better than fish, eh, matey?" Ros asked, munching on pieces of the captain. Ros's face was Technicolor mold—an autumn of reds, browns, and golds.

"*Arrrrr*," I said, tilting my head to the side and squinting one eye closed in the universal pirate face.

"*Arrrrr*," Ros replied, baring his teeth.

Shiver me timbers. Yo-ho-ho and a bottle of rum. I was a parrot-on-the-shoulder, peg-leg, skull-and-crossbones badass motherfucker.

Shit, pirates ain't got nothing on us zombies.

AFTER OUR MEAL, we regrouped on the poop deck. Ros was lying on his side, picking his teeth with a piece of wood. He pulled out a black molar and threw it into the lake. A bird landed on the railing of the boat, some water creature with stilt legs and a long orange beak. She looked at us with eyes blank as a zombie's; no one moved to eat her, full as we were with dead flesh. She squawked once and flew off.

Judging from the sun and the mildness of the wind, it was early spring.

Joan made a noise like a drowning cat and took off her waterproof backpack. The top was ripped open, the zipper broken. She turned it upside down. Water, brine shrimp, and plants tumbled out, but no Isaac. In the passion of our feeding, we'd forgotten him. Where was our red-eyed devil baby? Guts ran to Joan and pounded his fists on her squishy bosom.

"In the lake," Ros said. "But not dead. Never dead."

Ros was right. Isaac would wash up on shore one day, ravaged by the lake and its fish, perhaps little more than a skeleton, but ravenous nevertheless.

Brains, Part II: Isaac's Revenge.

We all looked rancid. Annie's cheek had a gaping hole ringed with brown blood and leeches; Ros was missing a few fetid fingers, probably eaten by fish; we all carried snails, weeds, shells, and clams in our hair and pockets, clinging to our clothes and flesh. Joan stuck a finger in her ear and out popped a minnow. Guts picked the weeds out of her eyeball.

"What's the plan, captain?" Ros asked.

Wavelets slapped against the stern or the bow or the fore or the aft. The clouds looked like ducks or demons or Africa. In between them, a plane flew.

It had been a cold winter for zombies. If planes were flying.

I stood up and removed my water gear. Time for a checkup; everyone did the same. We formed a circle and examined each other. Guts's guts were gray worms; Ros's ribs poked through his chest and the tip of his penis was gone; moss was growing on Annie's stomach. What looked like cottage cheese covered Joan's chest, and all of our hair was falling out.

I was afraid to look down at my own body, although it had betrayed me long ago. I nodded at Joan and mimed sewing, taping, healing.

"First aid kit," Ros said. "Down below." Joan saluted and turned on her heel.

It took hours to save us, from flies and their maggots, from fluvial decay and skeletonization. Saint Joan worked on each of us in turn. Guts helped her, scraping rot like barnacles, sewing up holes, and wrapping tape around softening bones. Guts found a paint set somewhere below and with it, Joan became an artist as well as a mortician, coloring our faces with pinks, peaches, and browns, reddening our lips. Preparing our bodies for viewing. Or for war.

Joan sewed a tarp over my torso; it crinkled when I moved, but it was firmer than my own flesh. I fiddled with the boat's radio. The battery was dead. I found a few guns under one of the cots. Although Annie was shell-shocked, more Annabel Lee than Annie Oakley, she smiled at me when I pressed one of the guns into her hand, and that old light gleamed in her eye; she wasn't totally gone, not yet. I set an empty water bottle on the edge of the ship. Annie took aim and nailed it.

"Atta girl!" Ros said. "Knew you were in there." Joan was fitting a pair of pantyhose over his ribs; she paused to smile maternally at Annie. "Where to?" Ros asked.

I gestured at the horizon as if to say, "Wherever the wind takes us, soldier boy, whichever way the wind blows."

"Roger that," Ros said.

After we were all patched up and dressed—praise Saint Joan, miracle worker—Ros and I hauled anchor and the boat headed west with the wind, chasing the sun and the Joads and the stars in Hollywood. Our own Manifest Destiny.

Guts hung over the edge of *Maria Sangria*, scanning the water's surface for Isaac. The rest of us joined him. The sun was setting, turning the shifting clouds orange. It looked unreal, like an orange juice commercial or a glossy ad for a subdivision built around golf.

Ros spread his arms apart. "I'm the king of the world!" he yelled.

We all got the reference. Titanic. Gigantic. The future's so bright, we gotta eat brains.

Over half-decayed and Ros was still a clever boy. Iceberg of America, here we come.

CHAPTER TWENTY-ONE

THE WATER WAS all kinds of blue, the blue of cleaning fluid and electric Kool-Aid, the blue of the American flag and Indian belt buckles, the blue of the blood pooled in the bottom of a corpse. It glinted like diamonds as we headed west.

Go in one direction long enough, and you're bound to get somewhere. Even if it's right back where you started.

Because it's the journey that counts, isn't it?

"Who do you think is left?" Ros asked, rolling on the deck like a rag doll, as if his bones had liquefied. And maybe they had. "Man or zombieman?"

Annie tossed a frying pan in the air and shot it. "Hey!" Ros yelled. "Bullets don't grow on trees." She pulled off her middle finger and gave it to him.

"I get it," he said, scratching his cheek with her finger. "Very funny. But just more work for Joan."

Annie grabbed her finger and stomped over to Joan, her bitten ass a gelatinous mass of jiggle. She glared at Ros while Joan sewed the digit back on.

Guts shrieked and scrambled down from the crow's nest, binoculars hanging from his neck. He pointed west and handed the binoculars to me.

Chicago was in the distant horizon. The skyline looked like a diorama of a skyline; the antennae on top of the Sears Tower looked like cockroach antennae.

Chicago. Where Stein lived and died, and last we checked, where zombies ruled.

"What's out there?" Ros asked, reaching for the binoculars. I gave them to him. "Holy shit," he said. "The Windy City. How the fuck did we end up back here?"

Full circle, I wanted to say.

And wherever you go, there you are.

Ros offered the binoculars to Annie, but she wouldn't take them. She clutched Joan instead, burying her head in what was left of the matron's bosom, which was clad once again in the nurse's uniform. The two of them headed below deck.

We had time before we hit the shore of Lake Michigan, and I had to prepare for what we might encounter. If zombies met us, I would recruit for the revolution, the next step in our evolution, using simple illustrations like a newspaper comic strip.

It was more likely, however, that humans would be waiting with bullets and bombs, Rambos with ammo belts crisscrossing their bare chests, hell-bent on our destruction. For their own preservation, of course, and who could blame them?

We all want to survive.

I shuffled below deck with the women. I was looking for paper and cardboard, markers, paints, and pens. Writing is my superpower and it would save us.

Like the old IBM command goes: Think.

OUR BOAT SAILED toward Navy Pier as if someone were steering. As we drew near, the humans spotted us. Guts was in the crow's nest—he loved it up there, alone with the wind—when they sent up a flare. Guts fell down the mast and thumped on the deck, a puddle of slime forming immediately under his head.

"Incoming!" Ros cried, and giggled.

So far, so good.

To our right was a vintage lighthouse, to our left an oversized buoy. The sun reflected off the lake, turning everything into cardboard cutouts. Behind the pier were the skyscrapers, as ruined and vacant as Mayan temples.

I looked through the binoculars. The Ferris wheel stood motionless; the funnel cake and postcard stands were empty. At the end of the pier, where once upon a time tourists stood admiring the view, was a human male with his own binoculars, staring back at me.

I waved my arm for everyone to hit the deck. Guts stayed down with his slime and Ros joined him. I gave the human the thumbs-up, praying that my thumb looked like his—normal, pink, alive. The male returned the gesture and smiled. He looked truly happy to see what he thought were survivors. Who knew how many of them were left? Judging from the lack of activity on the pier, not many.

And then Annie emerged from the cabin.

As in: *She Came from the Grave*. As in: *She-Zombie from Below Deck*. As in: *Yacht of the Living Dead*.

She was armed with what we found on board—which wasn't much, but she still looked ready for battle. The human lowered his binoculars.

"Get down!" Ros said, and I complied. Ros with his metal head might be safe, but the rest of us had left our helmets back in Wisconsin.

We heard shouts from the humans—indistinct and urgent commands planning their attack, plotting our demise.

Guts whimpered and I put my arm around him. He nestled his head in my armpit, his hair one giant knot. I rolled onto my back and Guts curled against me like my wife. My head hit Annie's foot; her legs were apart like a commando's and she had the rifle at her shoulder, waiting to get close enough for a shot. I tugged on her pants, trying to stop her.

Because this was not how it should end.

"You go, Annie," Ros said. "Get 'em!"

There was the classic sound of a missile whistling overhead like a Wile E. Coyote Acme bomb, and the back of the boat exploded. Annie dropped to her knees; Saint Joan came stumbling out of the cabin, her bun charred and covered in dust.

I crawled over to the cardboard signs I'd made, gathered them under my arm, and pointed to the crow's nest—at an angle now as the boat started to sink.

Those signs would save us. Words and signs and symbols prove our intelligence; they create our consciousness.

Language isn't a virus from outer space, as Zombie William Burroughs said. It's a virus from within.

Like the zombie virus, it changed us. With language, we evolved.

Oh, that mad genius Stein; he was Copernicus, Darwin, and Einstein all rolled into one big 21st Century Fox.

Quick as a lick, Guts was on his feet. Running was his superpower and he used it for the good of the group. He grabbed the signs out of my hand and headed for the crow's nest. He climbed up the pole and with his brave little hands held the first sign high over his head.

WE CAN THINK, it read.

A bullet plowed into Guts's shoulder. He jerked back but continued to hold the sign aloft.

Language, our only savior. My words as revolutionary as the Magna Carta, the Treaty of Versailles, and *The Feminine Mystique*. The Declaration of Independence and the Bill of Rights.

We hold these truths to be self-evident: All zombies are created equal.

Guts moved to the second sign.

"What do they say?" Ros asked.

Guts held the sign up.

FRIEND? it asked.

And with that, they blew his brains out.

GUTS FELL INTO the lake, slow motion, end over end; the two signs followed him, floating down like paper airplanes. They bobbed on top of the water, impotent symbols with no one to read them, alphabet soup. The third sign landed on deck.

Annie gurgled and vocalized—"MROOOHAAA"—and charged

the bow, not even bothering to aim, shooting wildly at the shore. They shot her in the center of her forehead, right in her third eye.

Joan cried out, her grief palpable. With the young ones dead and Isaac at the bottom of the lake, our future looked nonexistent.

I crawled over to the only sign left—WE ARE YOU, it read. I clutched it to my breast as if it were the holiest relic, the shroud of Turin, a tortilla imprinted with the Virgin's face. A lock of Muhammad's hair.

"Holy shit," Ros said. "Plan, captain?"

I tossed him the binoculars and motioned for him to use them. Ros poked his metal head over the railing.

"They're huddled in a group," he said, "talking and pointing and looking over here. Barking into walkie-talkies. People running around too. With clipboards and shit." Ros lowered the binoculars and turned to me. "Getting pretty close to shore," he said. "Be face-to-face soon."

The boat was sinking, but the tide and the wind kept moving us westward. Flat on my stomach, elbow over elbow at zombie speed, clutching the final sign, I reached the bow and placed it on the railing.

"WE ARE YOU!" I wanted to shout it from the treetops: Just as humans came from apes, we came from humans. We are your descendants; that makes you our ancestors. Our fathers and mothers.

No one is alone. We are all connected.

The wind blew and pushed both the sign and boat forward; I held steady. They had to know.

A loudspeaker crackled.

"Attention," a voice said. "This is Lieutenant Bill Davis of the provisional United States Army. Surrender your weapons."

"Not very friendly," Ros said.

Joan grabbed the rifle out of Annie's cold dead hands and pulled herself over to me, resting the weapon on the railing next to my sign.

The object and its representation. The thing and its sign. The gun and the word.

Sticks and stones may break my bones. . .

I put my arm around Joan. Our healer, our saint. The goddess who kept us alive—yes, alive, not undead or living dead or stenches or corpses or rotters, but living beings.

Cogito, ergo sum. That's Zombie Descartes, of course. I think, therefore I am.

"Stand up," Lieutenant Davis commanded, the PA distorting his voice. "Stand where we can see you."

I shook my head at Joan. My eyes were pleading with her because her eyes had light in them, were filled with love. Like the first time I saw her, months ago, when Ros caged her like cattle and I rejoiced to find another like me.

"Don't stand," Ros said. "They'll shoot you."

Joan stroked my hair, a chunk of which came out in her hand. She tried to smile, I could tell, but her face remained immobile, a death mask.

I heard violins swelling as Joan rose to her knees; we all winced when her suede-covered bite site hit the deck. She put her hands on the rail and hoisted herself up to stand on the bow—a matron, a caretaker, everyone's mother. And without a doubt, a zombie.

She flashed the humans the peace sign.

"Identify yourself," Davis said.

She pointed to my sign. WE ARE YOU.

Somewhere on shore, a bazooka discharged, followed by a smattering of bullets. The boat rocked and Joan almost lost her footing.

"Hold your fire!" Davis yelled.

What a coward I was, hiding from the humans, cowering behind the wooden planks of the boat like a child under the covers, afraid of the dark. Joan looked down at me and this time she did crack a smile. The clouds shifted or the sun moved or the earth tilted and a halo formed behind her head.

From her nurse's pocket she removed a handgun, stuck it in her mouth, and blew her brains out. Her eyes never left mine.

Saint Joan, sacrificial lamb, she was stronger than we were. She refused to be captured by the enemy; she remained the mistress of her own fate.

Ros and I wailed; we ululated like Middle Eastern women whose children have been killed by taxis. Joan and the handgun and my sign fell to the deck.

"Get Stein," I heard Davis bark. "Now!"

My stomach jumped at the mention of our creator. I felt Lucy's sweet meat moving inside me. And Pete's brain in my bowels and my boss's pudgy flesh and A. J. Riley's bullet-ridden cerebellum. Every human I'd munched on, all the entrails I'd savored, they were a part of me now, as integral as my own intellect.

Ros clutched my sleeve. "Stein?" he said. "Pete said he was dead."

The stern hit the bottom of the harbor. The boat stopped sinking and settled. There wasn't much separating us physically from the humans now: the bow, twenty feet of water, and the pier. Ontologically, there was a chasm: beating hearts, digestive tracts, and sexual reproduction; architecture, Hello Kitty, and barbecue pork rinds.

But under the right conditions, zombies have something humans will never have: eternity. And at that moment, we had hope.

Howard Stein was coming in our greatest hour of need. He was a man of reason. A scientist. Surely he believed in Enlightenment ideals. Surely he'd help his creation.

"What should we do?" Ros asked.

I held my hand up, palm facing Ros, the traffic cop's signal to wait.

"I should try to talk to them," he said.

I shook my head no.

"But once they know I can speak, they can't kill us."

I didn't trust the military. I remembered Hurricane Katrina. Those Americans could speak. In fact, those Americans held up signs just as I had. Stranded on rooftops, the floodwater rising. Help us, the signs said. Save us.

"Can they?" Ros asked, rubbing his hands together, worrying them. "Would they?"

I put my hand on Ros's shoulder and nodded.

Tuskegee, Guantánamo, the crucifixion.

Ros stood up and saluted. "Private Drake, reporting for duty, sir!" he shouted, his voice deep and wavering, an underwater tuba.

Drake? To me, he'll always be Rosencrantz.

"Stand down, private," Davis said into the bullhorn. "Get back on deck."

Ros slumped next to me. "They don't care," he said.

A helicopter circled us. I looked through my binoculars at it and saw someone looking back. The hunter and the hunted; the gaze and its object; exhibitionist and voyeur—I didn't know which one I was anymore.

"Wish I still had on my uniform," Ros said. "That would show them."

I grabbed my sign; it was wet and limp, the letters blurry but still legible. I held it up for the men in the helicopter.

WE ARE YOU. That statement should end all wars: Christian vs. Muslim; White vs. Black; North vs. South; Bear vs. Shark. Us vs. Them.

Zombie vs. Man.

The helicopter hovered for a moment, then angled left and flew away. The first streaks of red appeared in the clouds, bathing Joan's splattered brains in crimson. Behind the skyscrapers, the sun was setting.

I took out paper and a pen. It was time to finish my masterpiece.

CHAPTER TWENTY-TWO

THE STARS LIT the sky like so many dynamos. The electric glow of Chicago was lost to the postapocalyptic power-plant shutdown; the lap of the water lulled Ros into near-catatonia. He was drooling in the bright moonlight, his vacant eyes closed in an imitation of sleep.

As for me, I worked on my treatise: *A Vindication of the Rights of the Post-Living.*

Because this was America, the City on the Hill, where everyone's inalienable rights were endowed by their creator. And my creator was on his way.

Let justice roll down like water and righteousness like a mighty stream!

I saw the boat approaching and my shoulder tingled, but I ignored them both, intent on scribbling the letters and words that represent the greatest concepts we can imagine: democracy, truth, equality.

"Hellooo?" a voice called. "This is Dr. Stein. Are you friend or foe?"

Ros stirred and tried to stand but I blocked him with my arm.

"Friend," Ros said.

"Man or zombie?"

"Zombie."

"Can you be both?"

Ros stood up, turned on a sloppy dime, and saluted. "Private Dennis Drake, reporting for duty."

"Mother of God," another voice said, and I heard guns being cocked.

"No need to overreact, gentlemen," Stein said. "I don't expect any trouble from these zombies."

I gathered my courage, tucked away my document, and made my stand next to Ros. Dr. Stein was perched on the bow of a sightseeing boat, the kind that takes visitors on sunset tours around the lake. He was surrounded by men with guns. A cane rested between his legs like a third limb, both his hands gripping the top. His hair and beard were long and white. He looked like Walt Whitman or Father Time.

I held the sign in front of me like a life preserver. A light shone on it.

"We are you," Stein read, and chuckled. "I suppose you are."

"Yes, sir," said Ros.

"And who are you, exactly?" Stein asked.

"Just me and the captain left, sir."

I threw my shoulders back and nodded at Stein, looked him square in the eye, communicating that we were both men of letters, rational, well-bred.

"There were more?" Stein asked.

"All dead."

"But *you're* dead, aren't you, Dennis?"

"Just a little." Ros looked at me. His eyes were hungry, desperate. "Pete said you were dead," he continued, licking his lips with his dry stick of a tongue.

"Rumors of my death have been greatly exaggerated. The more recent myths have me turned into the king of zombies. I've also been thrown from a fire escape and eaten by infected dogs." Stein paused. "Who's Pete?" he asked.

"Nobody. Anymore."

"For someone just a little bit dead, you're in remarkable shape. Do you have a doctor? A caregiver? Someone responsible for your upkeep?"

"Nurse. She shot herself in the head."

Stein bowed his head in sympathy. "I'm sorry for your loss," he said.

Ros pulled me down behind the railing. "Help me," he whispered. His eyes were yellowing like an old newspaper. He curled into a fetal position. "Brains," he whined.

I put my sign aside and embraced Ros. My brother-in-arms. My only friend.

Stein tapped on the boat.

"Private Drake," he called, "can I assist you in any way?"

Ros stood up, clicking his heels together. "Brains!" he wailed, and buried his face in his hands.

"There, there," Stein said. "It's not your fault. This should calm your stomach. For now."

He threw Ros a calf's liver and Ros shoved the whole thing in his mouth. Blood dripped on my head, and the killer inside me roared.

"I have something for your friend too," Stein said.

I am not your trained monkey, I wanted to shout. I am a PhD!

Nevertheless I stood up and held out my hand like a beggar.

Oh, humility! This was the moment when I should hand Stein my treatise; we would match wits and establish sympathy; empathy, love, and protection would be born. Cheeks would be turned, neighbors loved, peace agreements signed.

The American dream realized. Its promises fulfilled.

No such luck: Stein tossed me some pig intestines and I stuffed them in my mouth the long way, not even bothering to chew, sucking them in like linguini.

"Let me tell you a story," Stein said, "while you dine." He cleared his throat. I didn't look up from my meal. "Once upon a time," he began, "there was a scorpion, and this scorpion asked a fox to carry him across a rushing river.

"'But you'll sting me,' the fox protested.

"'If I did that,' the scorpion replied, 'we'd both drown. Since I need to cross the river, it wouldn't serve my interests to sting you. Have no fear. I'll refrain.'

"The fox agreed. He certainly couldn't argue with the scorpion's logic. But a funny thing happened: Halfway across the river, the scorpion stung him anyway.

"'Why?' the fox asked as they both drowned.

"'It's my nature. I'm a scorpion.'"

I stopped swallowing.

"You boys are scorpions," Stein said. "Do you understand me?"

I understood: Dogs chase cats. Bees make honey. Humans wage war. Zombies eat humans. No free will. And no compromises.

There was an old lady who swallowed a fly. We all know why she swallowed the fly. And now she'll die.

"There have been others like you," Stein said.

"I know. I collected them," Ros said, his face bloody. He looked like a greeting card photo of a baby covered with spaghetti sauce, the bowl on top of baby's head, a few noodles hanging down, and a caption reading: *I Didn't Do It!*

"Each of you proved the viability of my theory," Stein said, "that no one has to die."

"Where are they now?" Ros asked.

Stein made a sweeping gesture with his hand, as if the night held answers. As if the man in the moon cared. "My son," he said, "nothing has worked out as planned."

The best laid plans of mice and men . . . again and again and again.

"It was to be a new beginning," he continued, the cane impotent and resting against his leg. "Not an army of automatons or an enemy of man, but a new race, one with the potential to live indefinitely. One that wouldn't require food or shelter or gasoline or television. One that wouldn't waste natural resources." Stein looked up. "The virus wasn't ready when they unleashed it. Not even close." His eyes shone in the flashlight beam. They were the brown of mud, of dirt, of the clay with which he made us.

"Dr. Stein," one of the soldiers said with a note of warning in his voice, his eyes and rifle trained on Ros, who was twitching and contorting and moaning. Falling into character. Becoming the scorpion he was.

Stein shook his head, clearing it. "The military wanted to ship you to the desert. Turn you into soldiers for their war. But all hell broke loose first."

"Father," Ros gurgled.

"I have failed miserably. Our only choice is to give in, give up, submit."

"Save . . . us," Ros said. He grabbed my hand and held tight.

"It's too late for that," Stein continued, rubbing his forehead with his hand. "You're both prime specimens, and at first we tried to help your kind. We sought you out and brought you to our labs. We conducted experiments using positive and negative reinforcement, trying to teach you right from wrong. We had some success, but, well, Private Drake here, his behavior is typical."

Ros glanced my way; his eyes were as yellow as stomach bile. He was vibrating, a Holy Roller about to speak in tongues, the secret language, the word of God.

"BRAINS!" he yelled, and catapulted himself over the bow, heading straight for Stein.

It was a graceful dive, a swan dive, Olympic worthy. The soldiers opened fire; bullets pinged against Ros's metal trapdoor of a head and bullets penetrated his cranium, but Ros continued flying, free as any bird. And Stein, our father who art an old boob in a boat, stood up with open arms to receive him.

Ros knocked the mad scientist over; they landed on a bench seat, Stein bent over backward like a doll, embracing Ros, and Ros was really dead now, his brains scattered into the lake, no better—or worse—than chum.

Food for the worms. Ashes to ashes. The great beyond. A better place. Doggie heaven. All that rot. Pun intended.

I took a step back. Two soldiers tended to the good doctor; the remaining three turned to me, guns, rifles, pistols cocked.

"I'm fine," Stein said, pushing Ros's corpse off of him and standing up. "How's the other one?"

I held my hands over my head as if I were being arrested. The classic pose of submission. I raised one finger in the air and slowly moved my other arm. From my professor pocket, I pulled out my treatise, holding it between two fingers. I shook it at Stein.

"Looks like someone wants to tell us something," a soldier said.

Stein gave me the once-over, taking in my tattered tweed jacket and tarp of a torso, my pus-filled skull of a face, the rusted sores and scant strands of hair, and the crumpled and water-stained piece of paper in my hand.

"You think you're different, don't you, son?" he said, crossing his arms over his bulletproof vest.

I unfolded the paper and held it out so that the words faced Stein, as if they were an incantation or a spell. The password primeval. The sign of democracy. Somewhere in the city, there was an explosion and a barrage of machine-gun fire. The soldiers tensed and a radio squawked.

"Let's hope so," Stein said, nodding at the men. "Bring it here."

One of the soldiers approached me, and I smelled his brains, his musk, like fresh-baked bread, wild honeysuckle, Sunday-morning bacon. His helmet was too big for him; it covered all of his head and most of his face too. I didn't dare look at his eyes. I extended my arm and he snatched the document.

Stein put on a pair of reading glasses and sat down. "'A Vindication of the Rights of the Post-Living,'" he said. "'By Professor Jack Barnes.' Impressive title."

I lowered my head in a gesture of modesty.

Stein skimmed my manifesto, nodding his head occasionally. "Justice," he murmured. "Equality. True democracy. Hmmm. An analogy to slavery and suffrage. Very well written, Professor Barnes. Displaying a high degree of memory and cognition. There's no denying your intelligence."

Stein pointed to a passage near the end. "Here's the part that disturbs me, though. The part that punches a hole in your argument," he said, looking at me from over the top of his glasses. " 'Life, liberty, and the pursuit of brains,' " he continued. "Why did you write that, Jack?"

The soldiers laughed and stuck their arms out, murmuring, "Brains, brains," in a cruel parody of my people's behavior. I put my hands together in the prayer position.

"Enough!" Stein said, and the soldiers stopped clowning. "I can't stand to look at him anymore. Standing in front of me like a supplicant. As if I can protect him. Look, Jack, here's the cold truth: You're a by-product of biological warfare. A high-functioning by-product, but a by-product nevertheless. You're a mistake. Something out of *Frankenstein*."

I fell to my knees.

"You and I are mortal enemies," Stein continued. "And your compromise solution is absurd. We can't allow you to eat any of us because you won't stop there. Can't you see? If you're the lion, then I'm the gazelle. You're the spider; I'm the fly. The scorpion and the fox. No matter what you do, no matter how well you write or reason, you will always be a scorpion."

So words mean nothing: Freedom is the same as chair is the same as love is the same as Fruity Pebbles is the same as justice.

There's only one word with any meaning and I willed myself to say it:

"Braaaaaains!" I howled, and the effort hurt—my diaphragm, my throat, my stopped and broken heart.

From behind me, as if resurrected by my miraculous utterance, there was a banshee yell, a war cry, and Annie, dear undead Annie, came charging up the little hill of the half-sunken *Maria Sangria*.

Their bullet had entered her forehead and come out the other side, blowing her top off, exposing and cracking her skull like a pistachio. But her brain was intact and her aim was true. She shot the soldier closest to me in the neck and another in the eye. Two down, three to go.

The gunfight raged around me, but the soldiers were focused on Annie. I climbed onto the ledge of the boat and jumped, flying through the air like Superman.

I landed on Stein and we rolled on the bottom of the boat. The soldiers were yelling who knows what. Their sounds were as meaningful as birdsongs. A third fell dead into the lake.

Stein and I were in the missionary position with me on top, drooling contamination into his beard. I placed my hands over his ears and looked into his eyes. I imagined I was hypnotizing him like Dracula; I imagined Stein fell in love with me.

"I'll help you, Jack," he said. "There's a cure. Please. You can be human again!"

A cure? I don't need a cure. I'm perfect as I am. As God made me. As you made me, Dr. Stein. I am more than the sum of my parts, more than my hunger and the meat inside me. My soul is large; it contains multitudes.

Saint Joan's suicide taught me: I have a choice.

And I choose brains.

I opened my mouth wide, my breath filled with the stench of the grave. My bottom teeth sank into Stein's eyeball and my incisors punctured his brow. I bit down, shaking my head from side to side like a dog with a chew toy, working my way through the bone until I freed a chunk of his forehead. Then I sat back on my heels and chewed. And then I did it again. And again. Next to me, Annie was chomping on a soldier, her guns holstered.

The sky was lightening. A vulture landed on *Maria Sangria* and others circled overhead. I took another bite of Stein, eating his godhead, savoring the divine flavor.

It wasn't the Last Supper for Annie and me; it was the first.

EPILOGUE

ANNIE AND I—our bellies full for the time being, content, the top of her brain glistening like Jell-O in the dawn's early light—together we figured out how to start up the touring boat, and we hauled ass out of Chicago. Any minute, they'd come looking for Stein, but they wouldn't find him. He's in me. He's in you, too, if you accept him. He's in all of us.

We traveled north just as Ros had broadcast from the Garden of Eden, a couple of fresh corpses in the boat with us for snacks. Stein said there were others like Annie and me, and I believed him.

Professor Zombie finally had a viable plan: Find the others and work together to build a community. A resistance movement. A zombie underground in the cold, where it was dry as a morgue, where we'd be preserved.

I imagined we might travel to the desert one day, after the war was officially over and the humans felt safe again. After we ran out of food up in Canada or Alaska. I liked the sound of Death Valley, drier than dust. We could go anywhere we wanted. Once you accept your destiny, once you make peace with your nature, anything is possible.

Annie grabbed my arm and pointed to the east. Something was bobbing on top of the water and we headed for it, following a sunbeam. As we drew closer my heart swelled, almost started beating again; hope lodged in my throat like a large intestine.

It was Isaac, of course. The little Moses, floating on top of the lake like a rubber duck. We fished him out and unwrapped his waterproof covering and he was perfect, no worse for the wear, intact from head to toe. Like all babies, he was a tiny miracle. He squealed, gurgled, cooed. I brought him to my chest and Annie danced with her guns like Yosemite Sam.

I placed Isaac on one of the bodies and he dug in, using his sharp teeth and nails to peel back the skin. He must have been starving; he opened up the soldier's stomach and crawled in, then ate his way out like a maggot.

Annie took the wheel and redirected us north. I put my arm around her and with my other hand made a fist and raised it over my head, sounding my barbaric yawp over the roofs of the world.

The fish answered. And Annie and Isaac and the vultures and the flies, all of God's creatures together in one mad, inarticulate cry: brains.

ACKNOWLEDGMENTS

THANKS TO LAUREN Rosenfield, who came up with the title one hot night when *Brains* was just an idea, and Ted Frushour, who discussed key plot points and a variety of endings with me, none of which made it into the final draft. Special gratitude goes out to Truman State University's Sigma Tau Delta chapter for asking me to be their keynote speaker one spring and for agreeing to my lecture, "The Ontology of Zombies." Preparing for that talk crystallized my research and ideas, and I was encouraged by all the zombie-loving kids who attended the event.

Kenton DeAngeli whipped the manuscript into shape, forcing me to think big-picture hero cycle. I am forever indebted to Janet Reid, the funniest and sharpest agent on the planet, plus she eats brains for lunch. Thanks to Gabe Robinson for loving all things zombie and for curbing my bloody, gross, pun-loving side.

Special love to Sparky Romine for shopping, talking, rocking, and drinking. You are the best BFF a girl could ask for and I don't deserve your continued support. But I'll take it.

Finally, the best for last, my genius of a husband, Mark Spitzer, who taught me how to write by example . . . every day. Thanks for watching all those zombie movies with me, honey. You are a star.